**Marianne woke** [...] **of a smoke alar** [...]

Panic thrumming through her veins, Marianne leaped out of bed and snatched her robe. Throwing it on, she dashed into the living room. The room was dark but she could see the thick smoke. Her panic intensified as she realized the apartment was on fire.

Coughing and choking, she schooled herself to remain calm as she made her way to the front door. She hadn't reached the chain when she was grabbed and roughly shoved against the door. The man was taller than she, dressed in heavy clothing, the kind firemen wore.

"Where is the photo?" he demanded.

It was true what they said, she did see her life flash before her. Unable to scream because of the gloved hand over her mouth, sure she was going to die of smoke inhalation, she began to struggle. She might die, but it wouldn't be meekly.

## ABOUT THE AUTHOR

Last summer's family vacation was pure inspiration to Cathy Gillen Thacker. As she, her husband and three children were milling about an amusement park, the idea for this Intrigue was born. What would happen if someone went into the park and didn't come out? *Fatal Amusement* is the answer.

## Books by Cathy Gillen Thacker

### HARLEQUIN AMERICAN ROMANCE

37–TOUCH OF FIRE
75–PROMISE ME TODAY
102–HEART'S JOURNEY
134–REACH FOR THE STARS
143–A FAMILY TO CHERISH
156–HEAVEN SHARED
166–THE DEVLIN DARE
187–ROGUE'S BARGAIN
233–GUARDIAN ANGEL
247–FAMILY AFFAIR

### HARLEQUIN TEMPTATION

47–EMBRACE ME, LOVE
82–A PRIVATE PASSION

Don't miss any of our special offers. Write to us at the following address for information on our newest releases.

Harlequin Reader Service
901 Fuhrmann Blvd., P.O. Box 1397, Buffalo, NY 14240
Canadian address: P.O. Box 603,
Fort Erie, Ont. L2A 5X3

# Fatal Amusement

**Cathy Gillen Thacker**

*Harlequin Books*

TORONTO • NEW YORK • LONDON
AMSTERDAM • PARIS • SYDNEY • HAMBURG
STOCKHOLM • ATHENS • TOKYO • MILAN

Harlequin Intrigue edition published July 1988

ISBN 0-373-22094-4

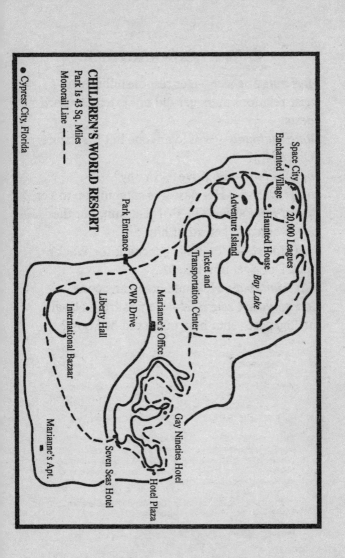

# CHILDREN'S WORLD RESORT

Park Is 43 Sq. Miles

Monorail Line — — —

- Cypress City, Florida

Space City
Enchanted Village
20,000 Leagues
Haunted House
Adventure Island
Bay Lake
Park Entrance
Ticket and
Transportation Center
CWR Drive
Marianne's Office
Liberty Hall
International Bazaar
Gay Nineties Hotel
Seven Seas Hotel
Hotel Plaza
Marianne's Apt.

# CAST OF CHARACTERS

*Marianne Spencer*—Her responsibilities as guest-relations manager did not extend to *dead* guests.

*Doug Maitland*—Would anyone but Marianne believe him?

*Joe Maitland*—Fugitive . . . or spy?

*Nina Granger*—Her past was catching up to her.

*Bryant Rockwell*—The FBI sent him, but the navy wanted to get rid of him.

*Stan Howell*—Would his penchant for Wacky Duck Dolls get him killed?

*Billy Maitland*—He could crack any code.

*Commander Craig Keel*—He was from Naval Intelligence . . . but how much did he know?

# *Prologue*

The tall man threaded his way through the throngs of tourists in the International Bazaar. But unlike the tourists swarming around him, he had no interest in the world-famous amusement park. He was looking for a man. And a deal.

If all went as he and Stan planned, they would soon be living like kings.

He watched as a man in a red and white Coca-Cola shirt approached the doorway of Liberty Hall in the American Experience exhibit. Joe followed, casually casing the place. Two Children's World Resort security guards stood watch near the door. They were armed and alert. He swore silently, knowing he could afford nothing to go wrong.

His hand on the compact revolver in his pocket, Joe scanned the rotunda. Tourists stood elbow to elbow on the marble floor, some viewing the paintings on the wall. His quarry—the man he hoped to rob—was making his way around slowly to study the framed copy of the Declaration of Independence.

Joe opened his camera case and fumbled with his Nikon, lacing it around his neck. To his left, a woman walked into the rotunda, her walk quick, her posture defensive. Was she the elusive unnamed quarry Joe had been hunting? She was fidgeting nervously with her sunglasses and kept glancing at her watch, but she didn't go near the Russian he'd been following for weeks. Maybe she wasn't the one.

The woman stealthily made her way around the rotunda. More people were entering the building, crowding the large room. Then the auditorium doors slid open and people started pushing and shoving to get in and find a seat.

Joe hung back slightly.

The woman headed for the auditorium. But the man in the Coca-Cola shirt didn't follow. Joe paused, looking around, and it was then he saw Stan intently shadowing another man. This one looked to be an American—young, middle thirties, Joe guessed. Dressed in a lavender Van Halen shirt and baggy white trousers, sandals, no socks. He had black hair, pale skin. Who the hell was he and why hadn't Joe seen him before?

The guide directed the tourists to various aisles. Joe thought it no accident that the woman and the guy in the Van Halen shirt sat next to each other.

Stan took a seat behind them, in plain view.

Neither of Stan's quarry spoke.

Joe wished to hell he knew what was going on. He shadowed the Russian to another seat six aisles back, between two vacationing families. Why wasn't the Russian making contact with anyone? The drop was supposed to be here, now, according to everything they knew. The second theft, Joe and Stan had decided, would follow immediately.

The lights went out. The show began. Joe stared ahead, barely seeing the life-size robots of Tom Jeffer-

son and Ben Franklin; he couldn't afford to get involved in a patriotic perspective on American history.
He knew it would all happen in the dark. By the time
the lights went on again, major espionage would've occurred. And Joe and Stan—this time they'd both benefit....

He felt himself smiling. He couldn't wait.


THE WOMAN COULDN'T SHAKE the feeling she was being
followed. She was afraid to go on, afraid to leave.

She glanced at her watch, forcing herself to calm
down. The fireworks would be starting any minute. The
crowds would wander off in that direction. It would be
easy enough then for her to discover if anyone was
watching her, and if not, easy enough to bolt.

A burst of sparkling, multicolored lights illuminated
the sky. She started slowly for the exit, her feet clatter-
ing on the sidewalk. As she'd hoped, everyone else
seemed to be gravitating toward the center of the park.
Heaving a sigh of relief, she quickened her steps.

Around another turn in the path, past the Magical
Seas exhibit, past the Harvest Bounty building....

She was being followed.

In a panic, she began to run. Desperate to find a way
out, she headed for the nearest rest room. She rounded
a shadowy corner, past a landscaped area around a
building; without warning he was there again, in front
of her. He caught her up by the arms, hard.

"You!" he gasped.

Panic surfaced. "Let me explain—"

"Traitor!" he snarled.

Without warning, another man stepped out in front
of her. It was the Russian, and he had a small gun aimed
at her, a determined icy smile on his face. She opened

her mouth to cry out. But before the first man could react, the Russian's gun had come down hard on the back of his skull and he crumpled like a rag doll at her feet.

She bent to him, but was stopped by a fist clenched around the back of her neck. "You tried to set me up," the Russian spat out.

"No, I swear—" In a panic, she tried to squirm away. He held fast, the gun resting against her throat. And she knew she was going to die.

# Chapter One

"You've got to help me. I know something's wrong."

Marianne faced Doug Maitland patiently. As the senior manager of guest relations, she had soothed many a distraught tourist in her time. Though maybe none as handsome as the man before her. In his thirties, he had longish wheat-colored hair, a wide sensual mouth—which right now was compressed into a tight, unhappy frown—and penetrating silver eyes. Yes, he was attractive all right, disturbingly so. And dangerously close to losing what was left of his admittedly limited patience. "Okay, calm down, and start from the beginning," she advised tranquilly. "You arrived at Children's World early Monday."

Doug nodded. "My father got here Sunday night. He'd already checked in to the Seven Seas Resort Hotel."

"When did you last see your father?" Marianne made a few notes.

"Monday morning, shortly after I arrived." Hands in his shorts pockets, Doug stood staring out at the magnificent view of the forty-three-square-mile park—a little bit of paradise in central Florida, as the CWR brochures said. Doug sighed heavily and continued his explanation. "Dad was on his way into the park. I walked him as far as the connecting monorail. He was going to the International Bazaar to make dinner reservations at the Mexican restaurant for next Sunday night. It's his birthday."

"You didn't go with him?"

"No. I was tired. I'd been up all night—first working, then getting a late flight. I just wanted to crash when I got here."

"So you went back to your hotel room to sleep."

"Right. I woke up about nine-thirty last night. I remember I was surprised I'd slept so long. You see, my father and I were supposed to go to dinner together and see some of the park."

Marianne could see why he was concerned. It had been almost twenty-four hours without a word, a message from the older Maitland. That wasn't reasonable. Unless, as Doug insisted, something had happened. Something . . . bad. "But he never showed," Marianne said sympathetically.

"Right. Not yesterday afternoon. Not last night. Not this morning."

"Was it possible he came back, found you asleep and decided not to disturb you?"

"No. And if he had, he would've left me a note or something. Besides, I'm a light sleeper. I would've heard someone at the door."

Marianne was quiet, studying her notes. She hated to ask the next question, but she knew she had to. "Has he ever been . . . inaccessible before?"

Doug's eyes flashed, then narrowed. "If you're asking me if he's unreliable—"

"I guess I am," Marianne said in a gentle tone.

"No." Doug still glared at her, his jaw set. "My dad is the most reliable guy I know. He's one hundred percent Navy, you know what I mean? His word is his bond. If he says he'll be there, he'll be there."

"How old is your father? And how's his health?"

"Fifty-four. And he's in better shape than most men half his age, always has been. Why, do you think—"

"The heat in June can get pretty intense. Some people get sick from it, if they're out in the sun too long."

"Yeah, I know. I've already called all the first-aid stations."

"Nothing?"

"Not a word. He hasn't been there."

Marianne swore inwardly. She almost wished Joe *had* been sick from the heat—at least then they'd know why he had disappeared. She wondered if she should call the Cypress City police. "Do you have any pictures?"

"Just this one." The photo he pulled from his pocket was dog-eared and worn. Marianne glanced at an older gentleman in a Navy uniform, with gray hair and a ready smile. Next to him was another Navy officer— years younger, with a striking resemblance to Joe Maitland.

"That's my younger brother, Billy," Doug identified the second person in the photo. "The picture was taken when he graduated from Annapolis four years ago."

Marianne looked back at Doug, taking in the long hair, the vacation clothes, the laid-back air. He couldn't have been less military if he'd tried. "Have you talked to your brother?"

"I called him late last night in California. He hasn't heard from Dad, either, but he's due to arrive later today."

"Is there anyone else he might call?"

"Only my sister. And she was at work all day yesterday completing a project. I finally caught up with her this morning, but she hadn't heard anything, either."

"I see. Well, I don't know what to tell you—"

"Isn't there any way to find out if he left the park?"

"Mr. Maitland, June is our peak tourist season. We have between thirty and sixty thousand guests a day. We accept the tickets of people going in, but we don't track the guests going out."

Doug swore, his frustration evident as he knotted his fists at his sides. Marianne's heart went out to him. She could see how worried he was, how concerned. And yet, she also knew it was possible this was all some sort of misunderstanding between the two men.

Children's World was a safe family resort. Crime was virtually nonexistent there; their security and medical staffs were first rate. If something had happened in the previous twenty-four hours, Marianne would know about it. Choosing her words with care, she asked, "You're sure something has happened to your father? He's never done anything like this before? It's not possible he met an old friend or went somewhere else for the night?"

Recognition lit Doug's eyes. "If Dad had wanted to go home with a woman, he would've called me," he replied dryly. "We had plans, Ms. Spencer. Definite plans. It isn't like him to back out and not notify me."

"Well..." Marianne sighed. "I guess the first place to start is the first-aid stations. We'll recheck the logs, see if anything turns up."

Doug returned to his chair and sat down.

It helped marginally, knowing someone at CWR believed him and was trying to help. But it didn't help much. He just couldn't shake the tense, uneasy feeling. In his gut, he knew something was wrong or his father would've been back. He would've called him.

Joe had had the usual ID on him, so that ruled out sickness, in all probability. And the alternatives that were left weren't at all pleasant.

Maybe he'd been robbed, beaten up, left for dead. Maybe he'd been a victim of the type of random senseless violence that sometimes occurred nowadays. Or maybe the violence hadn't been so incidental and unpremeditated after all....

"WELL," MARIANNE SAID WEARILY, putting down the phone and closing the file in front of her with a beleaguered sigh. "I'm really sorry, Doug. I was hoping we'd be able to get to the bottom of this by now." But they'd explored every available route and hadn't turned up any news. "I really just don't know what else to do."

Doug knew she'd tried, but in this case merely trying wasn't good enough. "You want to know what you can do? You can find my father, that's what you can do."

Marianne stared back at him levelly, her composure intact. "Believe me, Mr. Maitland, we here at Children's World are trying." He said nothing in response and she continued soothingly. "Look, I know you're upset. In the same situation, I would be, too. But we have to look at the facts here. Your father hasn't been treated at any first-aid station. He made reservations at the Mexican restaurant for your whole family on Sunday evening, so he obviously accomplished what he set out to do yesterday morning when he entered the park."

"You're suggesting I'm making a mountain out of a molehill?" Doug snapped.

"No. I am suggesting it's possible we've both been too negative in our attempts to conjure up an explanation. I mean, maybe, just maybe, there is a plausible explanation. Maybe your father did meet up with an old friend. Or made a new one—"

Doug had to admit that was the only sensible explanation. Yet in his gut he just didn't buy it. His dad didn't do things like that. He'd never had an irresponsible moment in his whole life and Doug told Marianne so.

"Okay, I'll alert security with a general description and photo of your father. If he's here on the complex and he needs help, he'll get it. If he's been in any trouble, we'll find out about it. And I'll continue to have my office do everything I can to locate him. But that's all I can do."

Doug was silent. He knew she was right; they'd done all they could, and more probably. But dammit, he was so frustrated. And depressed. And scared. Marianne Spencer was uneasy, too. She might not want to admit it, might not want to allow herself to think the worst, but Doug knew she was thinking it down deep.

Doug had the feeling he could trust her. Maybe because she was the type of person who generally liked people, who enjoyed getting involved, helping others. She seemed reliable and dedicated to her work, open and honest. She was pretty, in an understated, healthy way. But her appearance was not what he wanted to think about.

Marianne was still watching him, alert to the changing emotions on his face. "Is there anything else, something you're not telling me?"

"Like what?" His voice was finally in control as he studied her flame-red hair and flawless skin.

She looked good in her CWR suit—efficient and professional. She'd been kind and considerate in her dealings with him, all things considered. But he also knew she couldn't begin to understand the inner turmoil he was feeling—no one could unless they, too, had been through something like this firsthand. And then there were the unresolved conflicts he had with his father, conflicts he still didn't want to dwell on, never mind discuss with anyone else.

"I don't know." She shrugged, her eyes never leaving his face. And he knew by the intuitive way she was looking at him she had picked up on something. Maybe it was what he hadn't said, more than what he had. "Did you and your dad have a fight yesterday morning?"

For a second Doug froze. No, they hadn't had a fight, but in the past had the two men been together any length of time at all, they would've. Doug had been depending on this time to be different. "No, we didn't argue." He got up, restless again.

In fact, that was the crazy thing about this, he continued thinking. They had planned the trip to effect a sort of reconciliation, to erase the bad feelings that had fostered between them for many years. It had been his sister's idea, and he and his dad had gone along with it. But he wouldn't get into this with Ms. Marianne Spencer. She might think Joe had run out to avoid conflict, and Doug didn't buy that. His father wasn't a man to avoid a fight.

"Thanks for the time." He reached over her desk to shake her hand, more than aware he'd probably worn out his welcome.

She returned the handshake affably, her grip sure and warm. "I'm sorry I wasn't able to find your father for you," she said sympathetically, standing and walking him to the door.

"So am I." Doug turned to Marianne. "But I *am* going to find him. One way or another, I'll get to the bottom of this." He owed his dad that much. Doug wouldn't let him down. Not this time. He'd find his father... or he'd die trying.

STAN BENT OVER the washroom sink, his body stiff and cramped from a night spent sleeping under a row of bushes. It had been a hell of a couple days. God knew once he'd realized who the criminals were he hadn't wanted Joe in on this. He'd done an about-face and tried to keep him out of it. In the meantime the information was safe. And therefore, so was the stupid young woman who had tried to pass it off.

Now... now Stan had to concentrate on getting himself out of the park. He had been afraid to leave the Enchanted Village last night, even at midnight. The KGB had followed him over on the monorail and had no doubt been searching for him throughout the night. Probably even this morning. One would be watching the gate; the other—the other would be inside looking for Stan.

Stan had to change clothes. He walked into an adjacent gift shop and bought what he needed: a polo shirt and a pair of shorts, a CWR cap and sunglasses. And last but not least, the bait—a simple red, white and blue CWR carryall with assorted souvenirs and a Wacky Duck doll sticking out prominently.

With a glance over his shoulder Stan walked into the rest-room, changed, and stuffed his dirty clothes into the bottom of his tote. Now he looked like every other tourist in the place. Maybe it was possible for him to get out of the park without being spotted. It was worth a try.

He had to talk to Joe about their next move—and the sooner the better. Their very lives depended on it.

DOUG PAUSED AT THE DESK of the Seven Seas hotel, his impatience with everything around him showing in both his tone and gestures. "Any messages? Doug Maitland. Room 316."

The clerk obligingly checked the mailbox. "Nothing for you, but this came for Joseph Maitland."

"When?" Doug looked down at the manila envelope in front of him. It was postmarked Washington, D.C.

"Late last night. It was supposed to be delivered on Sunday morning but there was some sort of mix-up. The courier apologized and said they would be glad to give you a refund if—"

"Thanks." Doug took the envelope, cutting off the clerk's apology, and started to walk away.

"Sir, you'll need to sign for the envelope."

He hastily scrawled his name and asked again, "You're sure? No messages for me or my father?"

The clerk checked the boxes for 316 and 317. "Not a one. Are you expecting any?"

"Yeah. I think my dad might call. I'll be in my room if he does. Be sure to have the call put through immediately."

"Certainly, Mr. Maitland."

Doug strode back out of the huge welcome hut, a two-story structure directly on the monorail line, and made his way to the building that housed his room. At the elevator, he looked at the envelope in his hands, curiosity eating him alive. Strangely, there was no return address. He knew, if his father were okay and if he returned, he would be mad as hell at Doug for opening his mail. But if he didn't....

Deliberately, he tore open one end. Seconds later he was staring at several pages of hand-lettered music. It was a very crudely done piano and guitar version of "Silk Stockings." Not exactly his dad's usual style, at least not the last time he'd heard his avocational country and western band. Scrawled on the top of the page was a note: "Show this to your son—the real musician. I'd like to know if he thinks it's publishable. Maybe a new career? At our age, we gotta do something, and maybe arranging music for groups like ours is the thing." It was signed by Stan Howell, Joe's fiddle-and-piano-playing buddy.

Doug smiled and shook his head in exasperation and bewilderment, returning the music to its package. He didn't know what to do with it: he was a trumpet player, not a big-band leader. What were his father and Stan up to now?

He didn't have much time to contemplate that because when he reached his room, he found the door next to his was ajar.

Doug's hopes rose. Maybe his father had come back after all. "Dad?" He pushed open the door.

For a moment he was motionless, the air stalled in his throat. The tight feeling in his chest intensified until it was near pain. And still he couldn't move.

The place had been trashed from top to bottom.

# Chapter Two

"Now do you believe me?"

Marianne stared at Doug Maitland. He was furious, upset. He had every right to be both. It was her job to inject calmness into the situation, but she, too, was fast becoming very nervous about the whole situation. "Look. Right now we have no way of knowing whether these two events are related—"

His brows rose. "Guests here get their rooms trashed every day?" he asked through lightly gritted teeth, mistaking her attempt to remain objective with a lack of caring.

"No, of course not," she amended quickly.

"How often does it happen?"

"I don't know."

Taking her arm, he pulled her aside, away from the Cypress City police and CWR security men sorting through the tumbled remains of the room. "Don't bullshit me, Ms. Spencer. You're the head of guest relations here. You know damn well."

He was right, she did. "We have a break-in once every couple of months. Generally because someone leaves a door unlocked or—"

"The door wasn't unlocked. My father wasn't careless."

"This could've been a coincidence."

"Not likely," the Cypress City police officer offered, stepping around the mattress ticking spread over the carpet. "Whoever did this was looking for something." He glanced at Doug. "Your dad in any kind of trouble, son? Gambling or loan sharks—"

"No," Doug said tightly, clearly affronted. "My dad's as straight-arrow as they come."

The officer weighed Doug's statement carefully. "What is it your father does for a living?"

"He's in the Navy. He has a desk job in Washington." Doug's reply was curt, his jaw set.

"Nearing retirement?"

The question seemed to strike a nerve. Doug was silent a moment, then he slowly nodded, his voice becoming softer, more subdued. "Yeah. The next year or so."

Was there a problem there? Marianne wondered, picking up on Doug's reticence to discuss it. And why could that be?

"A lifer." The police officer smiled.

Pride tinged Doug's voice as he said, "Yeah."

Another plainclothes detective from Cypress City came up to question Doug. "Your father got any enemies you know of?"

"No." Doug took a deep breath and exhaled very slowly.

"Does he have something someone else might want? I mean, did he bring anything real expensive with him? Like jewelry or a gift?"

Doug was motionless for several seconds, then he shrugged helplessly. "Not that I know of. We've never been rich. Just the fact we're able to take a vacation like this . . . well, it's a first."

Without warning came the sound of footsteps, then an audible gasp.

Doug and Marianne both turned toward the door to see a husky young man in a Navy uniform in the doorway. Next to him was a bespectacled dark-haired woman in a business suit, carrying a briefcase in one hand, a tote in the other.

When she saw the destruction of the room, the young woman's face whitened treacherously. She looked helplessly at Doug, while the man beside her shook his head in mute horror and disgust. "My sister, Pamela, my brother, Billy," Doug mentioned in an aside to Marianne.

Billy let loose with a couple of swear words salty enough to burn the ears off a drunken sailor. "What the hell happened here?" he demanded roughly. Then to Doug, "Where's Dad?"

"I don't know." Doug started for his sister. Wordlessly, he welcomed her with a comforting embrace. "He hasn't been seen for over twenty-four hours now."

Pam slowly drew away from Doug. Marianne noted how frail she looked, how upset. She swallowed hard, and cast another look around the room, at the overturned chairs, the slashed pictures. "Doug—"

"It's going to be all right, Pam. We'll find him." Briefly, he explained what had transpired since he'd talked to them both on the phone. Pam seemed to recover as he talked about the efforts being made to locate her father.

Marianne, too, began to relax. She felt bad that his father was missing, but she knew that whatever happened next, at least Doug had his family around him.

The CWR security officer came forward. "We're going to have to replace the lock and the catch on the door."

Marianne nodded. "Anyone in the building see anything?"

The guard shook his head. "No, ma'am. Seemed to be business as usual. Whoever it was must've got in pretty quick."

"I guess so," Marianne murmured, perplexed. Crimes like this were bad for business. Normally CWR prided itself on having one of the best security systems in the country for a resort its size. But obviously, something had failed. And since the resort covered forty-three square miles and had fifteen large on-site hotels as well as two separate amusement parks, and wilderness campgrounds....finding the culprit would not be easy. It would be damn near impossible.

And it was June. Peak season. Sixty thousand guests visited CWR daily. What a time for trouble like this to happen. And she had the distinct premonition it wasn't over yet, not by a long shot. As apparently did the Maitlands.

Determined to do her job, she walked over to Doug and his family.

"Some family reunion this is turning out to be," Billy was muttering.

"I know," Pamela agreed in a strained voice. She took off her glasses and rubbed the bridge of her nose. "And it was all my idea."

"Which reminds me," Doug interjected, looking past his sister and into the hall. "Where's Seth? I thought he was coming in with you."

"He was, but he had a freak accident late Friday evening." She paused and exchanged commiserating glances with Billy, before turning back to face Doug somewhat reluctantly. "He was tired and in a hurry to get home and I guess he really wasn't watching what he was doing." Pam frowned, and finished in a tone that said it hurt her even to say it. "He accidentally slammed his hand in his car door."

Doug winced. "You're kidding."

"No, I'm not. And please don't mention it to him when he does get here on Wednesday. He's embarrassed enough as it is to have had such a stupid, clumsy accident. He's also had a lot of pain, and fifteen stitches."

Billy whistled and swore again.

For a moment, Doug was motionless, trying without much success to read behind the thinly veiled worry on his sister's face. "He's going to be all right, isn't he?"

Pamela nodded reluctantly, still looking as if she had a lot on her mind, her fiancé's health at the forefront. "Yes. He was just overtired. He's been working too hard lately—we both have—racking up a lot of overtime."

"Maybe this'll encourage him to slow down."

Pam shrugged. "I wish that were so but with our firm as busy as it is, there's not much hope for that. Not immediately anyway. As it is, when he does arrive, he's going to have to bring work with him."

"What about you?" Billy asked.

Pam nodded toward her briefcase and uttered a weary sigh. "I've already brought mine with me. Some vacation, huh? Having to spend most of the time cooped up in a hotel room working?"

"It'll ease up eventually for you, won't it?" Billy tried to take comfort where it could be found.

Pam didn't look very hopeful that would happen. Marianne knew how she felt. There were times when she felt too stressed, also, when she was buried in work, and during those times there was never any end in sight. At least not on an emotional level.

"Why didn't Seth just come down with you and bring his work with him, too?" Doug asked, still prowling around the room, looking for clues.

"He had planned to," Pam said, traipsing obediently after her older brother, "but that was before he hurt his hand. It was pretty stiff and sore, and he couldn't even begin to hold a pen, never mind actually write with one." She looked at her brothers' faces and smiled reassuringly. "Don't worry, he'll be here."

Doug turned to his sister and shook his head in relief and consternation, and then, unable to resist, he said teasingly, "I don't know, Sis. Sounds ominous. You know, like a sign. You sure you want to marry that guy?"

She smiled back, her eyes sparkling. "Quite sure. If there's one thing I know, it's that Seth is the man for me."

The police came forward to announce they'd wrapped up their investigation. "No prints, the room is clean, but I don't guess that's any surprise—it was a professional job through and through. Did you find anything missing, Mr. Maitland?"

"Nothing, so far as I could tell," Doug said, sifting through a stack of clean socks and pajamas.

"Okay, well, let us know if you do. Or if your father turns up. We'll want to talk to him, too."

"Thanks, I will."

"Is there anything I can do?' Marianne asked Doug. "Besides have the room cleared and set to rights."

He shook his head. "No. Except maybe have some-one at the desk be on the alert for any news from my dad. I'm going into Cypress City to file an official missing persons report in a little while."

"You'll let me know how it turns out?" Marianne asked. She wanted to help. She wasn't sure Doug was telling her everything, but it was clear now he had every right to be worried. And she most certainly didn't want any more violence or disruption on CWR property. Not if she could prevent it.

Doug held her eyes, assessing her candidly. He seemed to like what he saw. He also seemed vaguely discouraged. "Sure. Though they've told me they doubt much of anything will turn up. I've already checked the local hospitals—no one's seen anyone answering my father's description."

"There's probably a logical explanation for this," Marianne said firmly, wanting it to be true. But even knowing as little about Doug Maitland as she did, she couldn't believe his father would deliberately be so thoughtless. Not with children who cared so much about him, and certainly not on the eve of their pro-posed reunion.

So what was going on? And why was it happening at Children's World?

"LISTEN, YOU GUYS, just cool it now. I mean it. There's no reason to get so upset here," the young American whispered hoarsely, the sweat dripping down his brow in a steady stream. Mid-afternoon, the eleven-and-a-half-acre landfall known as Adventure Island was al-most deserted. Another ferry full of CWR tourists wasn't due for another twenty minutes.

The man-made forest was filled with chirps and tweets, hoarse caws and the lonely-sounding squawks of the peacocks. At the insistence of his companions, they had left the footpath and ventured farther into the undergrowth, stepping through dense ferns and flowers until they reached the shady, private nook created by a huge granite boulder and a dense thicket of bamboo.

"We will tell you when to cool it, Mr. Merchant," the blond KGB agent said, backing Tom up against the boulder, his forearm against his throat, expertly squeezing out air and leaving just enough—barely enough—to breathe. He held a gun against his temple, and the metal felt cold and deadly against Tom's skin.

The other Russian, the dark one with the receding hairline, moved in closer. With a sinister smile, he placed a small but lethal-looking ice pick against Tom Merchant's chest. One good quick stab, Tom knew, and it would pierce his heart. His heart would stop....

Oh, God, how and why had he ever gotten in this mess?

"You will tell us about yesterday," the blond agent demanded.

There was a sickening, too-sweet smell to the forest—an overabundance of flowers and fertile earth. "I don't know *what* happened yesterday," Tom choked out hoarsely, his voice as bewildered as he felt. The ice pick moved up his chest. The arm tightened across his throat.

"You tricked us."

"No! I swear. I—" He coughed and choked, feeling the arm tighten against his throat. Just when he thought he was going to pass out, the arm loosened again. His chest heaving with the effort it took to draw air into his lungs, Tom said frantically, "I don't know what happened."

"You are lying!"

"It's true. I don't. I took the drop from her exactly as planned. Exactly!"

"Yes. And then you lost it the moment you left the auditorium."

Tom swore. "That wasn't my fault. The man knocked me down. Didn't you see?"

"Where is the information?" They shook him roughly, slamming his head against the rock.

"I don't know," he gasped and then whimpered as pain rocketed through his skull. "I'm telling you—"

"Who was that old man?"

"I don't know!"

"If you are lying—"

The American swore again, more virulently. He struggled to be free and was rewarded with brutal pressure against his neck. He made several hoarse choking sounds. "I'm not lying." He dragged in a whispery breath, coughing and choking, aware he had never felt more panicked. "I swear it. I—look, I'll get you more information if that's what you want." His voice ended on a tearful plea.

The Russians exchanged glances. "We have already given you two chances." They seemed not inclined to give him another.

Tom felt his knees go weak. "Look, just give me time. I'll—we'll work out something."

"See that you do," the dark-haired man warned. "Because if you do not, Mr. Tom Merchant, we will kill you and your partner. It will not be quick or pleasant."

Tom believed him.

They released him and his legs buckled. Tom sank weakly to the ground and watched, tears of desperation blurring his eyes, as the two men departed as stealthily as they had come. He'd bought some time, but how much?

DOUG CAUGHT MARIANNE at seven o'clock, just as she was about to leave her office and call it a day. He explained about the package. "Anyway, it got me to thinking, maybe this friend of Dad's, Stan Howell, might know where he is. So I called him in D.C. I found out he's on vacation, too. Supposedly he'd told the fellows in his department he was thinking of going to Florida, too."

Marianne focused on the hope in his voice. "You think he might be here?"

"He might've showed up to surprise my father. It is Dad's birthday on Sunday."

"Stan and your father are good friends?"

"The best. They go way back. They went to the academy together, intelligence training, too."

Marianne's head shot up. Why hadn't Doug told them this before? "Your dad's a spy?" she asked, incredulously.

"No," Doug said, amusement showing on his face. "Not even close. Dad hasn't done any fieldwork for years. He's just a desk-bound guy nearing retirement. More like a department manager who juggles the budget and doles out assignments. So is Stan. Anyway, I thought I'd see if I could locate Stan. I've called all the hotels and I can't find anyone currently registered under Stan's name now. But that doesn't mean he doesn't have a reservation to check in tomorrow or the day after." He sat forward, a man with a very specific mission. "What I want to know is, is there any quick way to find out if Stan made a reservation here? None of the clerks at the individual hotels will check the central files, which I understand, but this isn't your average situation."

No, it wasn't, Marianne thought. And Doug wasn't the average man. There was something about him—a laconic, solitary air—kind of like the lone cowboy riding the range, tough and independent to a fault, the kind of man who felt deeply but no longer wore his heart on his sleeve—that got to her. It made her imagination and her feelings run wild. But that had no place in the business world, as she well knew, and she was a businesswoman first and foremost. She cleared her throat and kept her voice even as she responded to his query. "Well, there is a way to get that data, but I'm not allowed to give out that information."

"I understand, and I applaud your allegiance to your company, but these aren't normal circumstances. Please, Ms. Spencer. I'm at my wit's end, and so are my brother and sister."

Marianne hesitated. She knew how upset they all were, yet what he was asking her to do went against every rule. And she'd always been a person who appreciated rules and structure and the comfort of a serenely organized environment. But on the other hand, Doug was so desperate, so worried, and she had the feeling she could trust him, body and soul. What would it hurt to break the rules this one time?

"All right!" Marianne switched on the computer beside her desk and typed in the password that let her into central reservations. She tried several variations of Stan's name, but to no avail. "I'm sorry," she told Doug. "There's just nothing here."

Regret and frustration were plainly etched on his face. At that moment, she realized how very much it was costing him personally to remain calm, to keep his thinking ordered and rational, his spirits up.

She knew from his appearance earlier when he'd made his request that he was a very disciplined person and, from the way he dressed, something of a free spirit as well. There was something about the combination, coupled with his inner gentleness and the tenderness and caring he evidenced toward his family, his fierce sense of right and wrong, his inner drive and determination, that appealed to her greatly. Here at last was a man with principles, convictions that went soul-deep. "I'm sorry," she said again.

"So am I."

He looked so vulnerable at that moment Marianne wanted to reach out and touch his hand. But knowing that would be highly unprofessional, she remained motionless. She told herself sternly she couldn't afford to get close to a man who was going to be gone in a matter of days, because if there was one thing she wanted in her own life it was permanence, relationships that were enduring and not fleeting or secondary to everything else. Like jobs. And like it or not, Doug wouldn't be there long. In fact, she doubted she'd ever see him again once he left Florida. If the circumstances were reversed, she doubted she'd be in a hurry to go back to Children's World.

Doug was watching her, too, though what was on his mind exactly she couldn't say. It seemed likely he found her as attractive as she found him. And just as likely he wouldn't let anything get in the way of finding his dad, and that especially included the time out it would take to express a personal interest in a woman.

Marianne was glad for the interruption when the phone rang. She listened, then said briskly, "Send him in."

Looking up at Doug, she explained, "I put out the word on your father to all security personnel earlier this afternoon. They found a guard at the International Bazaar who thinks he saw Joe yesterday."

The guard came in, and without preamble, told them his story.

"It was during the fireworks last night, about nine o'clock. I thought I saw the man in the photo Ms. Spencer circulated. He was with another man and a woman."

Doug leaned forward earnestly, excitement etched on his face.

"The woman was blond. She wore sunglasses and a big hat. I remember the hat especially because the tall man—your father—pulled it off of her."

"Accidentally?"

"No, sir. He just reached up and yanked it off. She was kinda stunned. She opened her mouth like she was gonna scream or something and that's when I started over there."

"And then what happened?" Marianne wanted to know.

"Well, this other guy ran up and came to the lady's rescue. He clobbered your father on the head pretty good. Your father fell down—and the woman and the man took off. By the time I got there it was all over."

"Was my dad all right?" Doug said, worried and perplexed.

"Yeah. He stood up and, well, he was a little out of it for a minute, but then he was okay. He asked about the woman and I told her she ran off. And then he ran off. But it didn't make no difference, cause that man and that woman, they were long gone by then."

Irritated, Marianne demanded, "Why didn't you report this earlier. Or take the man to first aid?"

The guard shrugged. "They were gone before I had a chance to do anything."

Marianne and Doug sat there for several minutes in silence after the guard left. She felt restless and unsettled, and sorry for Doug and his family because of all they were going through.

He looked at her, reading her thoughts, though he assumed she was too well-bred to voice them. "No. As far as I know, Dad hasn't been involved with any woman. But I can't deny he's been lonely since my mom died a couple years ago. Or that women might find him attractive."

If the father was anything like the son, Marianne bet that was the case. Although why would Joe Maitland want to tear off any woman's hat? What the hell was going on?

She looked at him levelly. "Maybe that wasn't your dad."

"You heard the guard. He said he was sure."

"I also know it was dark. And that he'd want to be a hero—"

"It probably was my dad."

Marianne understood why Doug would want to latch onto the guard's report as gospel; it meant his father was at least okay physically. That he hadn't suffered a heart attack or been in a car wreck or anything. "Can you explain any of what he described?" She knew—on a purely logical level—they shouldn't be so quick to buy any of what they'd heard.

Doug sighed and looked confused and miserable again. "I can't. Not a single word." He buried his head in his hands and swore.

Marianne looked at him, wishing she had some comfort to give, something she could say, but at that moment she couldn't think of a thing. Then her phone rang again. *Please, let this be some concrete word on Doug's father. Let him be fine.*

It was security. Again. She listened, growing more and more white as the guard continued. "Yes. Absolutely. Close the ride and the whole area of the park. I don't know. Cite electrical problems, but just get the area cleared. I'll be right there."

Doug was waiting when she hung up, pacing back and forth like a caged tiger. "Bad news?"

Slowly, Marianne nodded. She'd wanted immediate redemption for Doug's father, but not this. Never this. As she faced him she felt tears of empathy filling her eyes. The last thing she wanted to do was deliver this kind of news; yet she knew she had to tell him. Her voice quavered slightly and she swallowed hard. "They've found a body floating in the 20,000 Leagues Under the Sea Ride over in the Enchanted Village." Dead, they'd said. No doubt about it.

Doug reeled backward, as if he'd had the wind knocked out of him. His face whitened, his eyes becoming unbearably grim and fearful. He looked like he might pass out. Marianne jumped out of her chair, and moving quickly to his side, helped him into the nearest seat. He accepted her help mutely, his expression still stunned and disbelieving and yet somehow, on some level, very afraid, too. His eyes never leaving her face, he asked hoarsely in a choked tone of voice, "Is it—"

Marianne shook her head and gestured helplessly. Her eyes brimmed to overflowing as she softly and reluctantly said, "We don't know, Doug. But the general description fits that of your father."

## Chapter Three

"Maybe you better let me handle this," Marianne said, as they approached the roped-off area minutes later. Although nothing had been resolved yet, she'd had time to get herself under control and she knew Doug needed her to be strong. He had continued to get whiter and quieter with every second that passed. It was as if he didn't trust himself to speak. She found herself wishing he'd babble incoherently or hysterically—anything but this tense, hurt silence. Instead, he merely sat next to her in the electric cart they'd used since entering the Enchanted Village, staring straight ahead, not really seeing anything. She wondered if it was memories he was lost in—or fear....

"No. I want to go. If it is my d—" His voice broke and he didn't finish.

Before she could even bring the cart to a stop Doug pushed out of his seat and ran toward the grisly scene at the edge of the ride.

The body had been mercifully covered with a blanket. The night had grown dark around them, and in the distance, in the sections of the park that had not been closed to the public, the evening fireworks were starting.

Doug winced as a particularly loud boom rent the air, then knelt to view the body. Slowly, the blanket was pulled back. Doug stared down into the discolored face of a fiftyish man with gray hair.

"This isn't my father," Doug said finally, clearing his throat, and heaving a tremulous sigh. "It's Stan Howell."

For a moment, Marianne was so shocked she couldn't speak.

She knelt on the other side of the body. It was unreal somehow, this whole episode, and yet it was all too real. There was a gaping cut and bruise on the man's forehead. His skin had a bluish cast.

"What do you think happened?" Marianne asked the security guard who'd first been called to the scene.

"More than likely he was just doing some overeager sight-seeing—hopped the fence and then slipped and fell. Probably struck his head on one of the metal parts of the ride that's underwater."

"Bullshit," Doug interrupted, coming up to join them. He looked furious, disgusted with Marianne and the guard. "Stan was no lawbreaker. He didn't just happen to hop a fence."

"Then how the hell do you think he got over here?" the guard shot back. "There's no way anyone on the ride can get out of those submarines. Nor can they lawfully roam around the compound. Look at it, man. It's surrounded by rocks, huge boulders. They're slippery as hell when wet."

Doug looked around, considered the guard's theory—a theory Marianne felt was very plausible.

"Please. Come over here and sit down." She directed him to a nearby park bench. The fireworks had ended, leaving that section of the park eerily quiet and dark.

Despite the heat of the night air, Doug was shaking. Shock, she thought. She went over to one of the paramedics and returned with a blanket to drape his shoulders. "Are you going to be all right? Do you want me to have someone see to you?"

"No. I just—I want to see that security guard we talked to earlier, the one who thought he saw my father arguing with that woman and another man."

"You don't think it was Stan—"

Doug shrugged. "At this point, I don't know what to think."

The guard, when called, rejected the idea it had been Stan with Joe. "The man I saw with your father was much skinnier, younger." But he didn't remember much else except that he'd been dressed in the usual tourist garb. Depressed, Doug thanked him and watched him walk away.

Marianne moved closer to Doug's side. The park would be closing in another hour. Although the monorails and buses back to the hotels and parking lots would be jammed until past one o'clock, she could get him out of there fairly quickly in the electric golf cart they'd come over in. "Do you want to go back to your hotel?"

Doug shook his head. "No. I want to see the rest of the investigation."

"Not much else to do tonight," the police officer said, coming back to update Marianne. "We'll need to send in some divers, to have a look around down there, but we'll need daylight to do it. We'll be back early—say at dawn?"

"Then I'll be here, too," Doug said. No way was anyone shutting him out.

"You don't have to do this," Doug said, as Marianne pulled her BMW onto the road to Doug's hotel.

"Sure I do."

"Because you want to see I'm given every consideration, or because you want me out of the way?"

Marianne had known from the start Doug was going to be a tough man to handle. He had that rebel look about him. It was in everything—the up-to-date clothing, the longish hair, the almost defiantly relaxed stance. What she hadn't bargained on was her reaction to him. The sympathy she'd felt for him earlier, the yearning to help him. And now—now she had the urge to somehow make him behave because she had the feeling that, as far as basic trouble went, she hadn't seen anything yet.

Marianne decided on a brisk, professional response. "I want you to be comfortable here, Mr. Maitland."

Doug flexed his shoulders against the back of the seat. His eyes remained straight ahead. "Yeah." His voice was underscored faintly with disbelief.

"Is there some reason you mistrust me?" she asked, slanting him a glance as she pulled into the Seven Seas hotel parking lot.

His response was simple and to the point. "I don't trust anyone." Not anymore...

Marianne followed him upstairs to the family rooms. She knew it was going to be difficult for Doug to alert his brother and sister to the news about Stan and she wanted—no, needed—to lend him emotional support. Doug called them all into his room and told them what had happened, as gently as possible.

"You can't possibly think it's murder?" Pamela said, beginning to shake. She was aghast at the news of their old family friend's death; tears of distress were running down her face.

Marianne knew how the other woman felt. She didn't want to believe the violence had happened, either. No matter why or how Stan had fallen into the ride, it had been a horrible way to die.

"What else could it be?" Doug asked simply, jumping to multiple conclusions, none of which Marianne thought were sound.

Billy looked wary. He was very quiet, having put his beer and his sandwich aside. "What are the police doing about this?" he asked Marianne.

"They're starting an investigation. They'll be sending divers down tomorrow morning at first light, to try to determine how or why—or even exactly where—Stan fell in."

Billy looked at Doug. "You don't think that Dad is— is dead, too?"

"I don't know," Doug said grimly. "But I'm beginning to get very worried."

So were they all, Marianne included.

"I'm calling Seth," Pamela said. "Work or no, he's got to get down here right away."

Moments later it was all arranged. There was no longer any reason for Marianne to stay, but she somehow felt reluctant to go.

"Well, if you need anything, you can call me. Any time." Marianne scribbled down her home number.

"I'll walk you down to your car," Doug said.

"Don't be silly, I—"

"It's dark. You're a woman alone. That's reason enough for me to go with you."

Marianne couldn't deny Stan's death had left her on edge—and that she'd feel safer in Doug's company. She smiled her gratitude and nodded her approval. He held the door and waited for her to go through.

A new tension existed between them as they made their way silently down the corridor. In an effort to fight it, Marianne attempted to dissect it. The circumstances of his father's disappearance, the continuing mystery, had thrown them together impossibly, the stress of the situation giving them intimate glances into each other's character. She'd seen him at his most vulnerable, and at his determined best. He'd seen her at her most tense, her most calm. She'd been there for him, as best she was able in the limits of her job, and in turn he'd been as cooperative as he was able to be. She was acutely aware of him, and not just as a resort guest whose family was in trouble, but as a smart, sexy man, a man who seemed to have it all together even under the worst of circumstances. And he was aware of her, too, seemingly on a very personal level. She saw it occasionally, in glimpses, what he didn't say as much as what he did.

It had been a long time since anyone had insisted on escorting her to her car, dark or no. She reveled in the feeling of being taken care of. It was hard to remain impartial as they walked the winding paths across the courtyard toward the parking lot. The night was dark and quiet. The pools were closed, as were all the snack bars and restaurants. Torches provided illumination, their open flames dancing in the wind as the breeze blew in softly across the lake, lending a romantic aura to the night.

She battled the illusion, reminding herself sternly that just a few short hours ago she had seen her first dead body. Perhaps her first murder. She also knew she felt strangely unsettled, that for the first time in a long time she wanted to cling to someone or something, and that Doug seemed to be feeling the same way. Anything to shut out the grisly reminder of what had just happened. Of what might come next. It would be foolhardy to give in to such an emotion, yet it was so strong, so compelling....as compelling as his virile presence.

Doug stopped next to her car, as unwilling to let her go as she was to leave. She knew how he felt. This went past simple awkwardness; there was no easy way for them to say good-night, not after all they'd been through together. And there was still so much unresolved, so many questions. She could see them in his eyes. And she knew also that at least half those questions pertained to her. What was she feeling? Where was this leading? Were they foolish to give in to it, foolish not to? The truth was they were still strangers on one level, and yet in many ways they were closer than people who had been lovers. She wondered then if he would ever forget her. She knew she'd never be able to forget him. Or this one moment in time. Because he was looking, abruptly, as if he very much wanted to kiss her. She knew she wanted to kiss him. If only out of curiosity, to find out if his touch would be as tender and kind and determined as the man himself...

"Thanks for being there for me tonight," he said softly, his eyes holding hers in a way that let her know he was still very much aware of her. "I know you went the extra mile for me and my family. I appreciate it." The speech was soft and to the point, meant only to thank, and yet it touched her senses through and through.

She started to duck her head shyly and turn away, wanting to run again. And then she felt his hand on her shoulder, simple and direct, turning her back.

She drew in a long breath and slowly looked up into his face. Without warning, all the barriers that had been between them came tumbling down. She felt something much, much deeper and stronger than simple compassion for him. And she knew then that this awareness between them would've sprung up no matter where or when or how they'd met; it was that elemental, that strong, that irrevocable.

Time seemed suspended. They drifted in the romantic aura of the night, the torchlight flickering around them, the warm evening breeze gently caressing their bodies. Try as she might to walk away, as she knew she should, she felt unable to do anything but feel the emotions swamping her. "I wanted to help," Marianne replied finally, surprised by the unexpected breathlessness in her voice, the treacherously weak and giving way she felt. Warning bells sounded in her head. Because of his sensual, mesmerizing presence, she was wearing her heart on her sleeve, and that was something she *never* did. Never.

His eyes darkened, his look turned reverent; he seemed to be reading what was on her mind, and feeling it, too. "You have helped," he said softly, "just by listening. Just by believing."

And then, head lowering, he gently touched his lips to her cheek. The caress was tender, friendly, testing; not the erotic invitation she knew he wanted to give, and she wanted to receive. Nonetheless, Marianne felt warmed by it. She'd been right in her initial assessment of this man—he was dangerous in so many ways.

"Good night," Doug said softly, releasing her with the same slow deliberation with which he'd taken her into his arms.

Marianne could do nothing but keep her glance stoic and accepting and echo him politely. What she really wanted to do was start over again, under an entirely different, normal set of circumstances, one that had nothing to do with her work or his father. "Good night, Doug."

She got into her car, aware he didn't walk off or stop watching her until she had driven safely out of sight.

It was going to be a hell of a long night, she thought ruefully. And an even longer morning.

"DID ANYONE EVER TELL YOU you're a pain in the neck?" Marianne said, hunching down beside Doug the next morning. Her tone was laced with good-natured aggravation. Doug Maitland was fast testing her authority, and CWR's, over him. Marianne didn't want to see him push it to the limit, because at this point she wasn't sure who, if anyone, would win. Right now, undue publicity or attention was the last thing they needed.

Indeed, the only thing they had going for them at this point was the time. It was barely eight-thirty, and the park—what was not roped off—wouldn't open for another half an hour. That gave her plenty of time to handle Doug Maitland. She hoped.

"All the time," Doug admitted unperturbedly. Unexpectedly, he stopped examining the rocky ledge long enough to squint a contemplative look over at her. "I suppose you want to be the next?"

"You're straight about that much."

He moved lazily to his feet. She followed, hating the fact he was now towering over her and that temporarily, anyway, he seemed to have the edge. She tilted her head back, to better see his face. "I've been asked by security to ask you to leave."

"Sorry, no can do," Doug said crisply, walking off.

Marianne followed, cursing him silently every step of the way. He had her cornered, and they both knew it. Were she to forbid him access to the roped-off area, he'd probably go to the press. And then they really would be in deep mud up to their chins.

"Doug—"

"No speeches, Marianne. No pitiful pleas on behalf of the park, okay? 'Cause I'm just not in the mood to hear them." He whirled on her, suddenly furious beyond measure. "I don't give a damn about Children's World. I just care about my dad. I want him back with us, safe and sound."

She could see he hadn't had much sleep, if any, the previous night. Still, she hated his condescending tone and couldn't keep herself from reacting to it. "How do you know that's what I'm going to say?"

His cynical smile deepened. "You're telling me it isn't?"

She was silent, then took a deep, enervating breath. He was every bit the wild card, the man she couldn't count on or figure. "Look—"

He cut her off rudely. "Not a word of Stan's death was in the paper this morning. Not a word, Marianne!" He stalked toward her, his low voice vibrating with rage.

She had to control him. Her job was on the line. Because if she couldn't hush this up, if the tourists found out . . .

He studied her, still fuming. "You know something's going on here, don't you? Don't you?"

"All right. Yes. We—we're prepared to admit that something extraordinary may have happened here."

He snorted with laughter, apparently understanding how far she was prepared to go. "Oh, that's generous of you, Marianne, very generous. Well, tell me this, have you checked the other rides? Have you searched for more bodies, because ten to one my father's—" His voice became choked. He refused to finish.

Marianne looked at the binoculars he had laced around his neck. What were those for? What was he planning now? She was aware she hadn't been nearly enough help to him, but dammit, it wasn't because she hadn't tried. With effort, she forced herself to relax, to focus.

"Look, Doug," she whispered soothingly, touching his arm. "I'm sorry." About Stan. About his dad. About the cover-up they all knew was absolutely necessary.

"Yeah, well, fat lot of good that does me!"

"You can't stay here," Marianne informed him firmly, her position unmovable. "The park is going to open in twenty minutes."

Doug was aghast. "Including this ride?"

Despite the prick of conscience she had—wasn't that somehow disrespectful to the dead—she nodded slowly. She had her orders. "The police divers have been at it since dawn. They haven't found anything to indicate foul play; neither have our divers. It looks like he just fell—"

Doug muttered a profanity.

She stared at him, used to his swearing, expecting his wrath. She repeated herself firmly. "You have to leave."

"And the press?"

"They'll be notified as soon as the facts are in."

"Meaning what? That they'll probably print an article on the back page."

Marianne was silent, knowing that was exactly what was going to happen. "If it was an accident, what good would it do—"

"You've just hit on the pivotal words, Marianne. If it was an accident. Well, what if it wasn't?"

DOUG MADE A TOKEN SHOW of leaving the area as requested, but he had no intention of going back to the hotel as Marianne had so sweetly suggested. For one thing, he wasn't needed there—Billy and Pamela were around to see if his father showed up.

For another, he was sure he had missed something at the 20,000 Leagues ride, and so had everyone else. No way had Stan just fallen in or been prowling around. Stan had followed rules, not broken them. He wouldn't have hiked a six-foot fence, surrounded by shrubbery, unless he'd had a damn good reason. So, there had to be something there that would tell why or give them a clue as to what happened. If only Doug could discover it, then they'd be on their way to solving this mystery. His dad had always said tenacity was at least half of everything. Well, this once in his life, Doug was going to be tenacious. He was not going to be a quitter. He was not going to give up, as everyone half hoped he would. He would hang on until he did find something. He would make his dad proud of him. And maybe— just maybe—he'd also save Joe's life in the bargain. Because Doug just couldn't shake the unsettling premonition that his father was in danger. Grave danger.

Fifteen minutes after the park and the ride opened up, Doug was standing in line for 20,000 Leagues. Acting as nonchalantly as possible, he got on, then, when sandwiched between two families and several squirming toddlers, he looked out the portholes of the underwater submarine at the scenery around him. He saw lots of floating objects—treasure chests, pirate skeletons, fish—but all were part of the ride. Nonetheless, he took the ride again, and then again, viewing the scenery first from one side of the submarine, then the other. Finished, he selected a good vantage point, the top of a nearby hill, and using his binoculars, surveyed the outside of the ride. He tried to figure out where Stan had jumped the fence but couldn't. Dammit, he thought, scowling irritably, beginning to feel the intense June heat rising from the pavement beneath his feet. None of this made any sense, and.... And apparently he wasn't the only one concerned. On a distant rise stood a thin man in shorts and a Coca-Cola shirt. He had what looked to be a transistor radio plugged into his ear. And maybe—maybe a microphone somewhere on his shirt; either that or he was doing a great job of talking to himself.

Excited at his discovery, Doug scanned the crowds. Moments later, he found what he was looking for. Another man—this one young and of medium weight and slightly above average height—standing at the end of the line to get on a ride. He was wearing a navy CWR baseball cap and had a transistor plugged into his ear. He occasionally seemed to be mumbling to himself, or, Doug thought, to his *partner*.

Heart pounding, Doug put his binoculars down and started to make his way toward the young man. He was halfway there when a feminine hand curled around his arm, halting his progress. "I called you a pain?" Marianne said, using the sweet voice that grated on his nerves like fingernails down a chalkboard. "I should have made that a triple pain."

Doug started to swear and pull away.

He stopped when a brash-looking Navy officer stepped next to him. "Hold it right there, Mr. Maitland."

"Doug, this is Commander Keel, from Naval Investigative Services. He'd like a few words with you," Marianne said, still holding her cool, fixed smile. She made it very clear he was embarrassing her and she couldn't stand that; what's more, she probably wouldn't very easily forgive him for it. Doug sighed. Such was life.

He turned in the direction of the two men he'd sighted. But by now both were gone. He swore again, knowing he'd lost them, and perhaps his chance to identify them, as well.

"We can go in an executive lounge not too far from here—at the top of the Cinderella castle," Marianne directed.

"Do I have a choice?" he asked no one in particular.

"No," Marianne and Commander Keel echoed in unison.

Doug went with them only because he was curious as to what Keel might know. Was it possible his dad was working on a case and had gone undercover? Was that why Stan had been here, too?

Commander Keel thought not. "Hell, no, they weren't working on a case. Those two? I'd have to be outa my mind to—"

"You're my dad's new supervisor, aren't you?" Doug asked. He knew from Billy that his father and Stan had been assigned a new commanding officer they'd both hated.

"Yes. Why? Does that surprise you?" Commander Keel snapped.

Only if he wasn't some admiral's son, Doug thought. Only if he hadn't gotten where he was by nepotism alone, because he couldn't have been more than thirty-four or -five. "You're saying there was no Navy reason for my father to be in Florida?" Doug asked politely.

"Stan and Joe have been doing desk work only for the past three years. I thought you knew that. And they haven't been doing that very good. They take the longest damn coffee breaks I've ever seen. They're way behind on their necessary personnel reports and appraisals—"

Doug felt his jaw jut out, and his hands curl into fists at his sides. So help him, Navy or no, he'd take a swing at that young officer if he said one more thing against his father.

Commander Keel seemed to realize this. Sobering, he tried to attack the problem more sensitively. "Those two were put out to pasture a long time ago. If your father is in danger, and frankly I'm not yet convinced he is, then it isn't because of a Navy matter. It's something personal."

Hardly personal, Doug thought. His dad had never been in any kind of personal trouble in his life. No, if he'd ever been in any kind of trouble at all, it was because of his job with the Navy.

"If it's not Navy, then why are *you* here, Commander Keel?" Marianne asked quietly, asserting herself. Doug shot her a grateful look. At the moment he could use all the help he could get.

"Because Stan worked for Naval Investigative Services—desk-bound and pencil-pushing, but NIS just the same. And his death was mysterious. We'll investigate and file a report."

"And then it will be the end of the story," Doug cut in, making no effort to mask his unhappiness.

"I hope so, yes," Commander Keel finished curtly. He took a hard look at Doug, reading his emotional state. "If you want my advice, lay low. Wait for your dad to get in touch with you. Hell, for all any of us know this could be a romantic matter."

Doug thought of the blond woman his father had been seen with but dismissed the thought. "He would've called."

"Maybe. And maybe not. You haven't been around your dad in a long time, Doug. He never talks about you."

That hurt. Maybe Doug should have expected it, considering the many quarrels he and his dad had engaged in over the years. The months and even years of stony silence. But dammit, he'd thought—hoped—all that had begun to change. Had he been wrong? Had he been fooling himself? What was going on? Realizing Keel had expected the jab to hurt, Doug refused to let the pain show. Keeping his voice level, trying to ignore the concern he saw on Marianne's face, he retorted, pleased he was able to keep the defensive edge out of his low civil tone, "Maybe he doesn't talk about me to you—"

"Not to anyone at NIS. Joe's private life was always his own. That's the way he preferred to keep it. With that in mind, I suggest you go back to your hotel and wait it out. Or simply enjoy the resort. As it is now," Keel finished smugly, "you're only in the way."

FOR THE SECOND TIME in twenty-four hours, Marianne found herself driving Doug back to his hotel. She tried her best to maintain a professional distance from him, but it was nearly impossible. He was clearly distraught, unhappy, worried out of his mind. And she couldn't blame him. If something had happened to Joe...

It hadn't. She had to believe that.

Back at the hotel, they had another surprise: Seth, Pamela's fiancé, had arrived. A serious-looking man in his late twenties, he had ash brown hair that was going prematurely gray. Like Pamela, he wore horn-rimmed glasses and had brought a briefcase full of work with him.

Pamela herself was looking poised and in control again, as if it comforted her to have her fiancé with her. Watching the two of them, Marianne had to admit she was a little envious. She longed for that kind of closeness, the intimacy, herself.

In fact, the whole group looked unaccountably happy considering the general circumstances, and Doug commented on it.

"Well, maybe that's because we're getting some genuine help from the authorities," Seth admitted with a relieved sigh.

"Seth asked his friend Bryant Rockwell to help us find Dad," Pamela said, also looking relieved.

"He's with the FBI," Seth explained.

Almost as if on cue, Bryant appeared in the doorway, waiting to be introduced. He seemed the quintessential yuppie, from his Brooks Brothers suit down to his wing-tipped shoes. "Seth told me about what happened to your dad," Bryant said sympathetically to Doug as they shook hands. "I'm sorry. If it's any comfort, I—and the FBI—will do what we can to locate him."

"Wait a minute." Doug was not at all pleased by this turn of events. "What does the FBI have to do with this? Do you think there's more going on here than we know?"

"That's my personal theory," Bryant said calmly but objectively. "Joe works for the NIS, so did Stan. Admittedly, they're both near retirement and have been doing mostly security checks and routine management chores, but they are also both privy to a lot of classified material, and they've both worked on a lot of highly sensitive material in their time. Joe could be wanted for that reason."

"You're saying you think he's been kidnapped?" To Doug, this was the first theory presented to them that made any sense.

Bryant nodded reluctantly.

"The NIS doesn't feel that way."

"Keel is a . . . jerk," Bryant said finally, and they all laughed, the tension in the room momentarily relieved by Bryant's frank assessment of Keel's character. "Anyway, Keel wouldn't be down here himself if he didn't think he had something to hide—or uncover. He would have sent one of his lackeys."

It seemed there was no love lost between the FBI and the NIS, Marianne noted dispassionately. "Doug's thoughts exactly." She sighed.

"So we're in agreement; we'll all work together on this to bring your father back safe and sound?" Bryant asked.

They all nodded. The matter settled, everyone opted for lunch, except Doug who was staying to watch over their rooms. Marianne prepared to return to her office.

"I'm sorry if I was a nuisance this morning," Doug apologized, one shoulder against the portal, his lanky body partially barring her exit.

Marianne didn't want to leave him, either; but she had a ton of work waiting for her, a boss to answer to, and heaven only knew what emergencies would be cropping up that afternoon. "I know you're worried," she said softly. *And I hope your father comes back safe.*

Doug nodded, still watching her, looking as if he wanted very much to kiss her again. *He just wants to forget,* she thought, *he wants to use the passion to buy himself a little time to forget. I can't blame him, not if I'm honest, but I'm not going to let him use me, either. Because that I won't recover from.*

She forced herself to concentrate on the situation rather than the man, and on her professional responsibilities. "If I do hear anything—the police have promised to get back to me the moment the autopsy report on Stan is in—where can I reach you?"

Doug shrugged. "I'll probably be around here most of the day. Billy and Bryant want the chance to get around and do their own digging, too. Who knows, maybe they'll pick up on something I didn't."

"And tonight?" Marianne asked, aware there was a breathless sensation in her chest she couldn't account for.

"I'll be over at the Starlight Lounge in the Vista Hotel." It was CWR's most elegant lounge. His eyes darkened as he studied the lines of her face. "I've got a gig there tonight," he related, his voice soft as silk on her ravaged nerves.

Marianne looked at him, stunned. Damn, but he was sexy when he wanted to be. And he knew it, too.

The shock—and displeasure—at his revelation hit her with tidal-wave force. It was all she could do to disguise them even partially. "You're a musician?" she asked in the most level tone she could manage.

Her dislike of artists registered. He nodded laconically. "A trumpet player. I thought you knew," he said slowly.

No, she hadn't known, Marianne thought. If she had, she never would have let herself start to get even this close to him. She would've kept a vast distance and made sure her guard was up at all times.

"My office has nothing to do with entertainment," she said. "Unless of course there's a complaint about one of the shows," she continued in a blasé tone. She gave him a sweet, meaningless smile. "Then I arrange refunds."

The lazy grin broadened and reached his eyes. They glinted at her, sultry and silver. "Well, let's hope you don't hear any complaints about my performance tonight," he said, straightening slowly and moving away from the doorframe.

She hoped she didn't, too, but for an entirely different reason. She didn't want to see him again. Not alone. Not in a crowd. "Right," she said briskly, edging around him without preamble and into the hall. "Well, I've got to go back to work. I'll be at my office. You've got the number, should there be anything I can do on your family's behalf." Maybe in the future when she dealt with the Maitlands she could deal with Pamela.

"And you'll call me with the results on—" Doug paused as another tourist passed "—Stan?"

She nodded, grateful he'd used tact and avoided the word autopsy in front of another tourist. "Will do."

## Chapter Four

"So, how are things going with the Maitlands?" Nina Granger asked later the same afternoon.

"As well as can be expected," Marianne said as she took a seat in front of her boss's desk and filled her in on all that had happened that day.

Nina nodded to indicate she was listening and lit a cigarette as Marianne finished bringing her up to date. When Marianne was done, Nina was silent. She looked thoughtful and unhappy. Marianne knew how she felt; she wasn't thrilled about the situation, either.

"What a mess," Nina said finally, in a flat, accepting tone.

"Agreed."

"At least the Maitlands haven't gone to the newspapers with any of this. You did impress the importance of that on them, didn't you?"

Unlike Nina, Marianne's first thoughts were not for the business they were running, but rather for the plight of the people she was trying to help. Especially Doug. But she also knew what was expected of her professionally. "I tried. They were unhappy about the cover-up of Stan's death, though."

"The Navy tells me that was necessary."

And of course Nina wasn't fighting it, because negative publicity would hurt the resort. And Nina wouldn't want that.

As the vice-president in charge of site operations, Nina was one of the few people on the site who did not have to wear some sort of uniform, and she dressed very well, in expensive sophisticated clothing. Her short black hair was styled in a wedge cut and she was thin to the point of anorexia. Single, she had few close ties. She didn't talk about her past—she'd been with CWR for seven years—and she had no family to speak of. Her only vice, it seemed, was her fondness for Virginia Slims cigarettes. Right after she finished one, she usually lit another.

"I want you to stick with the Maitlands. Especially the older son—what was his name?"

"Doug."

"Right. He's already been a nuisance. He could turn out to be a real blabbermouth."

Marianne had to suppress the need to defend Doug. Oh, she knew he'd been nosy, all right, but she also knew if she'd been in his shoes she would have acted precisely the same way. Nina, however, probably wouldn't have.

"Anything else?" Keeping her voice polite, Marianne rose and started toward the door.

"Just keep me informed. I want to know everything—and I mean everything," Nina finished emphatically.

Marianne stared at her boss. It wasn't like Nina to be so involved in any one problem, no matter how sticky. Of course, this was the first time they'd had a murder on the site. And though right now officially there was no connection between Joe's disappearance and Stan's death, they could be sitting on top of a scandal of mammoth proportions. Nina knew that, obviously, and feared it.

"Would you like to meet the Maitlands?" Marianne said slowly, wondering how she could ease her boss's mind and at the same time let her see the Maitlands weren't enemies but a nice family who needed their help.

"No. That's your domain, Marianne."

Marianne stared at her, perplexed. It had never been like Nina to be afraid of anything, yet she seemed afraid of this. "I just thought—"

"You handle the guests. I'll handle the mechanics of running this resort. I just want to be kept informed. At all times. Got it?" Her voice was gruff, not to be argued with.

Marianne nodded slowly. Why was her boss so touchy about this? Why was she looking so frightened suddenly? And why did she insist on remaining at arm's length from the Maitland family?

As it happened, though, Marianne had little chance to think about it further, for when she got back to her office, she found a phone message for her from Billy. She dialed his number. He answered on the first ring.

"Hi," she said pleasantly. "What's up?"

"Nothing good," he said grimly. "I'm afraid we've got more bad news."

DOUG WAS IN THE MIDDLE of his last song when he saw Marianne standing in the back of the nightclub. It was all he could do to finish the song, but somehow he did. When he headed backstage Marianne was waiting for him in the narrow hall that ran between the dressing rooms.

"We need to talk." Her eyes were serious, her face pale, her hands twisted into a tight knot in front of her.

A ripple of unease swept through him, ten times more potent than before. *Please, not bad news.* Grabbing her arm just above the elbow, he led her into the dressing room he'd been assigned, and shut the door behind them. He still held her arm, his grip almost desperate. "Have they—"

"No. There's been no word on your dad. But Billy called to tell me Pamela and Seth's belongings have been rifled through. I went over at once, of course." Seeing how worried Doug was, she sought to reassure him, "They're both understandably upset. I called in a CWR security crew as well as the Cypress City police to investigate. As far as Seth and Pam can tell so far, nothing is missing. And if it's a repeat of what's already happened—and it looks as if it is—I seriously doubt they'll find any fingerprints."

"Another professional job?"

"It looked that way to me when I was over there, yes."

Aware suddenly he was still holding on to her, and that her skin was incredibly soft beneath his fingers, Doug released her slowly. With more than necessary concentration, he took his mouthpiece out of his trumpet and placed it and the trumpet carefully in the case.

"How did it happen?"

Marianne was wearing her short-sleeved CWR uniform blouse, and a navy skirt and vest. The blazer she usually wore in her office was nowhere in sight, and she rubbed her hands over her bare forearms as if she were cold.

"Apparently, Seth and Pam went down to dinner. Billy was in his room keeping an eye on things and he fell asleep. For what it's worth, even though the robbery went on next door, he didn't hear a thing.''

The way things had been going, it figured. "So much for soundproofed rooms," Doug said dryly.

Marianne forced a half smile, appreciating his attempt to retain his sense of humor in the face of adversity. "I guess so."

Silence stretched between them. Doug knew he only had a few more minutes until his next show began. Suddenly aware of the intimacy of the small room—they could hardly move without bumping into each other—she eased away from him slowly, as if her muscles ached. "What'd you think of the show?" he asked casually. He wanted her opinion—maybe a little more than he should, he noted dispassionately.

For a moment, she didn't speak, then she paled a little and avoided his eyes. "It was great."

He'd read more enthusiasm in a negative review. He stared at her, wondering what was wrong. From where he'd stood, it had looked as if she were enjoying his music, caught up in the spell. Why was she denying it now? Could it be she was afraid of coming off like some groupie?

"Look, I've got to go." She turned and stepped past him toward the door.

"Sure you don't want to stay?" he asked, moving with her.

She stepped around him and pulled open the door. "Thanks for inviting me, but I've got a lot of work left."

The rejection couldn't have been clearer had she slapped him in the face. He stared at her, wondering what he'd done to deserve her disdain. It shouldn't have bothered him. Normally, he wasn't one to pursue lost causes. But in this case it did. Maybe because she seemed to be saying the opposite of what he'd swear her first reaction had been.

For some reason he couldn't quite identify, maybe didn't want to, he felt he had to pin her down. "You'll be at your office?" he asked casually.

"No. My apartment. It's quieter there." She hesitated, a guilty, uncomfortable look on her face. "If you or your family need any more help."

He knew when aid was reluctantly given, and again he wondered what he had done to turn her off. He watched her, his face guarded. "I won't hesitate to call," he promised quietly, his tone final. And this once he knew it was a promise he would keep.

NINA GRANGER KNEW she wasn't alone the moment she walked into her penthouse apartment overlooking the International Bazaar. Craig Keel was sitting in an armchair, a glass of whiskey in his hand. For the first time since he had arrived at Children's World, he was out of his Navy uniform, and he looked at that moment not so much like an officer, but an old friend.

He was also an unexpected and, at that moment, an unwanted guest. Nonetheless, she wasted no time asking him how he'd gained entry to her home. He was a master at everything associated with criminal activity and espionage—picking locks, planting listening devices.

Not bothering to turn on a light, she walked to the bar and deliberately poured herself a Scotch. "Anyone see you come in?" She knew her neighbors gossiped, and that she didn't need.

"You know me better than that." He gave her a familiar glance that let her know he still remembered the time when they had been lovers, and not just simply compatriots.

"What do you want?" she asked tersely, wishing he would leave. She'd put the past behind her, or she had tried to, and now with his presence he was dredging it all up again.

He studied her, obviously wishing for a warmer welcome. "Can't two old friends get together?"

"When it comes to the two of us? No. We can't."

He was silent, not disputing the difficulties that could crop up if they were seen together in an intimate setting. "How are things on your end?"

"Under control."

"You call three break-ins in twenty four hours 'under control'?"

Nina took a long swallow of Scotch. She should have known he'd know about that. She relaxed only slightly as the liquor warmed her stomach. "I'm doing what I can from my end to put a lid on it, Craig."

Craig knew her well enough to know that was true. In Washington, she had learned fast and well how to protect herself, and everything that mattered to her, including her own job.

"And Marianne Spencer?" he asked. "Where are her loyalties?"

Nina lit a cigarette. There was no use lying to him about Marianne Spencer. Although she was a likable enough woman, she could also be a major detriment to Craig's operation. Especially if she didn't like or trust him. "She tends to get overly involved in the people aspect of things." Nina took a deep draught of nicotine and chased it down with more Scotch. Having emptied the first glass, she moved to pour herself another two fingers. Nina hadn't felt this need to drink—and drink heavily—since she'd left Washington. Swallowing around the burning in her throat, she continued her assessment of her subordinate. "She's very concerned about the Maitlands."

"A soft touch?" He made a scornful sound. "I thought so."

"Of course, that's her job," Nina said unemotionally. "Catering to the needs of specific people. However, her efforts to make things easier for the family could inadvertently lead to a major disclosure of the trouble here." Which in turn probably meant excruciating trauma for them both.

He guessed her thoughts and agreed with them. "You'd end up in the limelight."

Nina nodded affirmatively, her countenance grim. "I am the senior CWR manager on site. And we both know my past can't bear scrutinizing." She gave him a hard look as he helped himself to more of her whiskey. He, too, was looking pale and uneasy. It was some comfort to her, knowing she wasn't the only person who was unnerved when confronted with a reopening of their notorious past. Consequently, she felt closer to him. "What about you?" she asked softly, feeling a sympathy that had been foreign to her for some time begin to reassert itself. "What about this Stan and Joe?"

"They've been nothing but deadbeats and dissenters since day one," Craig growled, pacing.

Nina stared at him. Realizing how edgy he was made her nervous. And when she got nervous she looked for someone to blame. "Then you should have gotten rid of them earlier," Nina said short-temperedly. If he had, neither of them would have this problem now.

"If you only knew how hard I tried," Craig Keel said dryly. "But they were wise to every one of my machinations, right from the start, and they didn't want any part of the early retirement I would have arranged for them." His mouth turned grim and unforgiving again. "Instead, they were always subtly undercutting my authority every time I turned around, challenging me."

Nina could see there was no love lost between Craig and Joe. With two volatile men on the loose, and a third already murdered, the potential for scandal was immense. She had to calm Craig down, make him see reason. "So what now?" she asked simply, knowing the lower the profile they both kept on this, the better.

"We find Joe—if he's still alive."

Nina's hands were shaking as she smoked her cigarette down to the butt and then smashed it out; she didn't like the vengeful look on Craig's face. "And then what?"

"He'll get exactly what's coming to him." Craig turned to her, letting her see he meant every word he said.

A shudder went through her; she suppressed it. "What if he's already dead?" she asked calmly.

More silence. He shrugged and said unemotionally, "Then there's nothing I can do."

Nina was silent.

"Until I can put a lid on this, it'd pay to be as careful as possible."

Nina agreed. She didn't want to go back to looking over her shoulder every minute. She didn't want to live her life in fear.

MARIANNE WAS STILL SHAKING when she got home from the club. She knew it was nerves, all that had happened to the Maitlands, that was behind her uneasiness. And yet it was more. It was Doug. She wasn't sure how or when it had started, exactly. At first she had seen him only as a guest with a problem. Oh, she'd known all along he was attractive, and that his character and personality appealed to her. But she'd had the constrictions of her job to help keep the barriers up between them, to help keep their association from turning personal.

With everything that had happened since, though, keeping the relationship impersonal had become an impossible task. She'd found herself caring about him, friend to friend, woman to man. She'd found herself caring about his family. She wanted to know more about him. Or she'd thought she did. Until she found out what he did for a living. Then, like it or not, she had realized with startling clarity that her original attitude had been the correct one. She couldn't get close to Doug. It was wrong. Anything beyond even a surface friendship would just never work. Not given the way she felt about artists in general.

When another half hour had passed, she knew she had sulked enough. Deliberately throwing off her low mood, she poured herself a glass of wine and ran a bubble bath. After a good long soak, she felt much better, revived, soothed. Unfortunately, her doorbell rang just as she was pulling on a nightgown and robe.

She tied the front of her robe shut and went swiftly to the door. Through the viewer she saw a grim-faced Doug Maitland standing outside. He looked . . . upset. Forgetting for a moment her decision to resurrect the barriers between them, she unlocked the door to let him in. "What's wrong?" she asked, hating the disturbed, angry look she saw on his face. Had something else happened in regard to the break-in? Had the police dis-covered some fingerprints after all?

"Nothing. Everything." He strode past her without waiting for an invitation.

"Has anything happened?" she asked, shutting the door and following him into her living room. She wished her cheeks weren't still flushed from the heat of the bath, that she were dressed. When she was with Doug, she needed every edge possible just to keep them apart.

He shook his head. "No, it's just that the waiting is getting to me." She motioned for him to sit down and he did so reluctantly. "The autopsy results on Stan aren't due until tomorrow. I talked to Commander Keel again tonight. He was at the second show. I think he was half hoping for my father to show up to see me play. Of course he didn't."

"Did you talk to Keel?"

"I tried. Not that it did me any good." Doug sighed his frustration, his dislike of the ambitious officer evi-dent. "He's keeping all his cards close to his chest."

Marianne studied Doug, wondering if it was only Keel that had him so upset. Or if there was something else, something more behind his restless mood. "You think he knows something?"

Doug shrugged to indicate he was guessing. "I'd be damn surprised if he didn't. But as for him sharing any of his suspicions with me . . . well, that's a false hope if there ever was one."

He sighed again, his agitation showing. He got to his feet again, his voice low and urgent. "Has Keel con-fided in you at all? Do you have any idea what he's up to?" Without warning, he bridged the distance between them and towered over her. "Marianne, please. I've got to know."

He was asking her to betray what amounted to professional confidences. "Doug, you know I can't—"

"If my father's life weren't at stake, I wouldn't ask you to."

She knew if the situation were reversed, she'd be doing the same.

Sensing he'd run into a dead end, he tried another tack. "Are there any other NIS men from Washington around? I'm not talking about the Navy divers or the lackeys he pulled from the local base—"

That she could answer. "Not that I know of, no."

"Don't you find that odd? That Keel came down here himself to do the investigating?"

"In a way," Marianne said slowly. "As high ranking as he is, I would've expected him to send an investigator or a team while he waited for the results back in D.C."

"But he didn't."

"No."

"Instead he's here personally. Right from the very beginning."

And he had put in a special phone line that allowed him to communicate with his superiors back in D.C. without fear of being overheard by any CWR operator. But she couldn't tell Doug that. She'd been sworn to secrecy by the government. The only reason she had known was because they had needed her—the CWR's cooperation—to achieve the task.

"What do you think about his feelings for Stan and for my dad?" Doug watched her carefully for any signs of evasiveness or duplicity. "Come on, level with me. Does he seem suspicious to you? Against them?"

"He doesn't have any sympathy for them, that's for sure," Marianne said, sighing. The mellowness she'd felt after her bath was gone. In its place was an edge of excitement, danger. The feeling wasn't altogether unpleasant.

"That's what I thought, too."

And about that there was nothing they could do. Nor could she seem to fight her growing awareness of Doug as a man. When he first came in, Doug had been too upset to notice the state of her undress. Now, however, they were both acutely aware of it, as well as the lateness of the hour, the intimacy in the dimly lit apartment.

She knew she had to get rid of him.

She moved away from him, her action a dismissal.

But he had no intention of leaving, not yet.

"One more thing. Earlier, at the lounge," he said softly, his eyes holding hers. He paused, his expression curious. "Did I do something to make you angry with me or upset?"

For a moment, Marianne didn't know what to say. She didn't want to tell him the truth or hurt his feelings. She didn't want to let him know how prejudiced she was. She didn't want to be aware of his quicksilver eyes, or his soft and silky wheat-colored hair. She didn't want to think about his tall, rangy frame, the loose, easy way he moved. She didn't want to think about sexy men with gentle eyes and fiery souls. "No," Marianne said evasively, wishing he wasn't quite so adept at reading her emotions.

He studied her again, then looked around her apartment, as if that would give him a clue, even if she wouldn't. Unfortunately, it did, and she thought she knew what he was thinking as he looked at the lemon yellow satin sofa and low-slung white coffee and end tables, the spinet piano with the single magazine rack of music beside it. There was a profusion of blooming plants—all pretty and fragrant. Sculptures in brass and crystal. All her magazines were tucked into white wicker baskets, her books arranged on white shelves on either side of the fireplace she'd never once had occasion to use. The whole apartment was ordered and neat—upscale, very settled. The abode of a very single, successful career woman.

She contrasted it with the vision of his home—if he had one, and somehow she wasn't sure he would have anything but a room here and there, knowing the life he lived. Everything would be replaceable, interchangeable. Except his music and his trumpet.

He turned back to her, his conclusion reached. "Is it the fact I'm a musician?"

His tone was silky, dangerous. She forced herself to look into his eyes. She knew then, as much as she wanted to, that she couldn't lie to him, or evade, not about this. Besides, maybe it was better he know, that she be honest. "Yes," she said simply, dropping her gaze.

He drew in a long breath, the depth of his disillusionment giving his voice an edge. "Let me guess. You don't consider it a 'real' job. Right?" Apparently he'd suffered this stigma before; he was angry and hurt, his eyes a deep glittering silver.

"No, it's more complicated than that." He knew she was embarrassed at having been caught with her prejudice showing; he wasn't going to bail her out. She moved away from him, running a hand through her hair. Her peignoir swirled around her ankles as she walked. "My father is an actor. He was never very successful when I was growing up. And as a result, the first ten years of my life were very tumultuous.''

The way he was looking at her made her shiver and set her teeth on edge. ''We moved around a lot,'' she continued, still pacing as restively as a caged tiger. ''We went from New York to Los Angeles, to wherever the work was the moment the next job came up, and sometimes when there wasn't any job, only hope.''

''You sound bitter.''

''Maybe I am. I missed a lot.'' And she hated sounding so defensive. With an effort, she lowered her voice and calmed down. ''My parents loved each other but they couldn't maintain that love during the intense pressures, the ups and downs.''

''You were in the middle?'' he guessed, his tone softening just a little.

Marianne felt her stomach churn, just remembering. ''Constantly,'' she admitted. It helped, knowing he understood this much about her. ''Anyway, when I was ten my mother divorced my dad and married a business executive. I hated her for it at first, because despite everything I still loved my father, but later I saw it was the best thing she could have done for me. For the first time in my life, I lived in a stable environment. I was able to go to school, not just for a few weeks at a time, here and there, but year after year in the same place. I was able to make friends. I flourished because of the security and permanency a steady life-style provided.'' And she'd never forgotten how good that had felt. Or how bad the unsettled life-style had been.

''What does any of that have to do with your getting to know me?'' he asked quietly.

''Everything and nothing.''

''I don't understand.''

"I want that kind of settled life-style for myself. I want marriage, children, a stable home."

"And you don't think you could have any of that with me?"

He knew she couldn't, although to even be discussing it at that stage was ludicrous. They barely knew each other.

"Let's just say I'm not going to waste my time looking for peaches on an apple tree." She sought refuge in a flip comeback.

"Ah, I see. Ever efficient, aren't you, Marianne?"

The edge was back in his voice, the unsettled feeling back in her middle. "Look, it's been a long day, and tomorrow promises to be even longer." Clutching the edges of her robe closed with a splayed hand to her throat, she stalked deliberately toward the front door. She still felt naked beneath his gaze.

His strides long and lazy, he moved with her, matching her every forward movement, not stopping until they were both standing right next to the door. Marianne was aware her heart was beating too fast at the sight of the predatory look in his eyes.

"Let me see if I understand this," he said silkily, letting his gaze rove her lips. "You're attracted to me, but you won't allow yourself to act on those feelings."

Determined to meet him equably, she snapped back, "That about sums it up."

Without warning, his arms were on either side of the wall beside her. "Wrong, lady. That doesn't begin to sum it up, because not everyone can compartmentalize their feelings as easily as you claim you do. Take me, for instance," he continued determinedly, his arms sliding down to close around her waist. "I can't separate my feelings into neat little categories. I can't feel something because I should, or not feel something because I shouldn't.''

"A pity." She wedged her arms between them and pushed, to no avail; he wasn't budging until he'd had his say.

"Is it?" he asked rhetorically, his warm breath blowing across her temple. "I don't think so. I think you're the one we need to feel sorry for."

"Doug—" She was breathless, resisting. And even as she damned herself for desiring him, her mouth ached to know his kiss.

"But then, maybe not. Maybe you're not as strong and unconquerable as you'd like everyone to think."

The wall was against her shoulders, the length of his hard body against her breasts and thighs. They seemed to touch everywhere, her thin gown and robe no protection against his strength or the desire pulsing between them. "Stop it," she said hoarsely.

For a moment, he stilled, staring down at her. She could feel his desire, and she knew he could see hers, in the frantic raising and lowering of her chest. She damned herself again for wanting him, for not being able to resist something she knew could only bring them both pain.

His gaze darkened. "Let's see how much you don't want me, Marianne," he whispered temptingly, his mouth poised roguishly over hers. With one hand he tangled his fingers through the damp ends of her hair. "Let's just see."

She expected his kiss to be harsh and demanding. It was soft and ravishing, reaching her in ways she hadn't known possible. Nonetheless, she fought him at first, splaying her hands across his chest, trying desperately—unsuccessfully—to keep them apart. His embrace was the whisper of a sunlit morning, the first summons of a potentially deep and everlasting love, and she was helpless. Similarly caught up, he murmured her name, once and then again. And then he was kissing her again, more passionately this time, without needing to prove anything or take, just to give. Desire fluttered through her and she opened to him, willingly this time. His hands drifted lower, to her shoulders, before coasting down her spine and pulling her closer. And still he kissed her, until her lips were soft and giving, her mouth open and accepting the rapacious sweep of his tongue. She tasted the bittersweet thrill of a love just out of her reach, she tasted him, she tasted desire. And she felt at that instant that she was beginning to know him, heart and soul, and that he already knew her—maybe all too well. That there were things between them that maybe always would be unresolved, and other things that had no choice but to reach a resolution of some sort.

When he released her long moments later, they were both shaking with reaction and pent-up desire. She stared at him, frustrated, aching, breathless.

He stared back, then looked at her steadily, as if to call her a liar. "Deny that," he said, and then without waiting for her to reply or defend herself, or even retract what she'd said earlier, he turned and wordlessly walked out her door.

# Chapter Five

"Thank you all for coming," Marianne said, as Doug and his family assembled in her office. Additionally, she had invited FBI agent Bryant Rockwell, her boss, Nina Granger, and Commander Craig Keel to hear the county coroner's report. All were grim-faced as she took a seat behind her desk and waited for the remarks of the coroner, an untidy officious-looking man.

"The official cause of death is drowning," he announced in an emotionless tone. "Although there were some irregularities."

"Such as?" Keel demanded, eyes narrowing.

The coroner sighed at the interruption, pushed his bifocals higher on the bridge of his nose. "Specifically, Stan Howell had sodium pentothal, or truth serum, in his blood. Furthermore, the placement of the needle marks on his arm would seem to indicate it was not administered with Mr. Howell's cooperation."

"I would guess not," Bryant said dryly, shooting the coroner a contemptuous look. Marianne readied herself to intervene if necessary. It hadn't taken her long to realize there was no love lost between the FBI and the Navy in this matter. They were fighting over every little bit of information, each one claiming jurisdiction, although, at the moment, no one really had a right to be there but the park officials and Cypress City police.

"What about the bruises on his face?" Keel demanded impatiently.

"The gash on his forehead was probably caused when he fell into the water. We're speculating he hit his head on the metal parts of the underwater ride, was knocked unconscious, then drowned."

"Anything else?" Doug asked, his expression frustrated.

The coroner nodded. "There was also some evidence to indicate Mr. Howell may have been chased over the fence that surrounds the 20,000 Leagues ride. He had scrape marks on his hands, stomach and one knee. Because of the drug in his system he was probably a little unsteady on his feet."

"You don't think he could have been pushed in?" Marianne asked. Her boss shot her a censuring look, which she ignored.

"There were no bruises on his arms," the coroner said.

"If he'd been pushed, he would've yelled," Bryant disagreed. "And no one heard anything, right?"

"Right." Marianne nodded. The ride's operators hadn't heard anything, but then it had been a very busy night. It had been getting dark. The ride itself circled around a three-acre lagoon surrounded by rocks and, above that, shrubs and trees and a six-foot security fence. And Stan had been found in the darkest furthermost section, between a large wooden section of wrecked clipper ship that stuck out of the water and the rock border of the lagoon. No, it wasn't likely anyone had heard anything. Even if Stan had shouted, with the sounds of all the children on all the park's various rides, it would have been regarded as just another shriek. In fact, if it hadn't been for a particularly observant ride operator, who just happened to notice a CWR cap floating in the water and walked around to investigate, the body might not have been spotted for hours.

"I don't like it. The whole thing stinks of murder to me," Keel said.

Nina Granger sent Keel a censuring look. If there was anything she didn't want, it was trouble for the park.

Bryant stood restlessly. "I don't like it," he said.

Nina Granger jumped in. "We've already got an agreement with the local paper. None of this will be reported."

Doug's head lifted sharply.

Billy concurred with Nina. "The less this is made public, the safer Dad is, Doug."

"I know it's hard for you," Pamela said, sensing her older brother's mood, "but it's important we cooperate with the police."

"Maybe if we put Dad's name and photo in the paper. Ran an announcement," Doug suggested. "Maybe someone would come forward to give us information on him."

"And maybe, just maybe, you'd be sealing his death warrant," Commander Keel said. He gave Doug a hard look. "Are you willing to take that chance?"

Doug wasn't.

The meeting disbanded with warnings for everyone to be careful. To Marianne's chagrin, Doug remained after everyone else had gone. Wordlessly, he got up to close the door behind them.

Marianne remained behind her desk, her heart beating fast. If there was anything she didn't want to discuss with him, it was what had happened between them the previous night.

He held up a hand before she could ask him to leave. "I know you don't have much time. I don't need much. I just want to apologize for what happened last night."

Marianne needlessly shuffled a few papers. She kept her tone and demeanor brisk. "That isn't necessary."

He sat on the corner of her desk. Ignoring her dismissal, he continued his apology softly, "That isn't the way I intended our first kiss to be."

She stopped shuffling. No doubt about it, the man was incredibly arrogant and self-possessed. But he wasn't the only one who could put on a good front. Her chin assumed a haughty angle. "But you did intend to kiss me."

His smile was slow in coming and very sexy. "Yes," he said softly, "I intended to kiss you. And I want to do it again."

Her heartbeat kicked in to triple time. She told herself she would not—would not—let him get to her again. But he was too close. Too appealing. She moved away from her desk.

"Doug, this isn't the time or the place—"

"I agree," he said, cutting her off. "And I promise, I won't violate the rules of appropriate conduct in a business setting. I did want to explain what set me off about what you said." He looked at her steadily, waiting for her permission to go on.

She knew then that there was more to what happened than she had allowed. "All right," she said slowly. "Continue."

"Being a musician can be both a blessing and an albatross. Women either come on to me—they're infatuated with what they perceive me to be, not what I am—or, like you, they detest what I do for a living, look down upon it, as if it's not a real job, not worthy of any respect."

"Doug, I didn't mean—" He played beautifully. His music had real artistry.

"If there's anything I can't stand from another person, it's smugness, the holier-than-thou treatment."

"That's what you thought I was doing to you last night?"

"Weren't you?" He gave her a level look.

*No. I was running.* But somehow it seemed safer to let him think her insensitive than to know the truth. She kept silent.

He came closer, until they were standing mere inches apart. Though Marianne was dressed in her CWR uniform, she felt no safer around him now than she had when she was dressed in a negligee. Maybe even less protected, because she knew that he did understand her, could see right into her soul, and that stripped her of her defenses. She didn't like being so vulnerable; it reminded her of her early childhood, and all the resulting pain.

"Look, before you knew what I did for a living, you treated me just like you would treat anyone else—a banker, an accountant, an insurance salesman. I liked that. I'd started to count on your friendship and support. Then when you found out I was a musician the change on your face was instantaneous. I saw this contempt—"

She couldn't help it. She didn't want him thinking the worst of her any longer. "It was fear. I just don't want to get hurt."

His gaze softened and he took her hands in his. "I wouldn't hurt you."

"I know you wouldn't mean to."

"There's no getting around this, is there?" He released his gentle grip on her hands.

"I meant what I said last night. I want permanency, Doug. I just can't settle for anything less. I'm sorry."

"So am I," he murmured, his look appreciative. He didn't look, however, like a man who was giving up.

Blessedly, the phone on her desk buzzed at that moment, interrupting them. Marianne walked over to answer it. She listened for several moments to the long-winded complaint on the other end. "All right, all right," she said finally, her normal patience gone. "I'll come over and inspect it right away."

"Trouble?" Doug asked as she hung up.

Marianne nodded. "There's a problem with the Space City ride. One of the maintenance workers says they're running the roller coasters too fast, that it's not only dangerous but it's making a few passengers ill. The mother of one of the sick children demanded he call the top manager—me, in this instance, since it's a problem with a guest—and explain the situation in her presence. So I'm going over to check it out."

"You look a little pale," Doug observed, his eyes dropping to her trembling fingers. "Is everything all right?"

"Of course," Marianne lied, then continued when he looked unconvinced. "We had this problem a few years ago. The lines for Space City get very long at peak season. People complain about waiting, so the crew responds by speeding the ride up. I'm not sure it's even a conscious decision on their part. Then people complain about getting sick. Then we slow the cars down, and people say we're running them too slow, that we've taken the thrill out of it."

"How often do you have to go ride it?"

"Only once a month or so." But that was more than enough.

"You hate roller coasters, don't you?"

"The truth? They scare the life out of me. And this one is even worse than usual because it's run almost entirely in the dark. It's neat, of course—it's like you're flying through the galaxy, with all the stars above, and on the sides you see what look like space cities. But—"

"It's fast."

Too fast for her taste. And they were running it continually at top speed—which meant about sixty miles an hour. She swore. There was no time for her to take a motion sickness pill; she'd be lucky not to get sick.

Doug was still watching her curiously. She felt his protective male instincts like a warm cloak over her shoulders.

"Want company?"

His question was no surprise. She also knew he needed a break, and that her boss would probably appreciate having Doug out from under foot for a while. Certainly the ride would get his mind off his dad, if only for a few minutes. "Why not?"

They entered Space City through an employees-only door, and went via a circuitous route to the head of the line. Marianne flashed her badge and spoke briefly to the crew chief. "Look, I know we've had a few people sick today."

"Yeah, well, if they are it's probably because of what they ate, or the heat." It was a scorching ninety-eight degrees, very sunny and humid. The chief pointed out the signs hanging overhead that disallowed children under ten and discouraged people with motion sickness from taking the ride.

Marianne, who was sympathetic to the employees who were doing their best to handle the peak crowds, nodded understandingly. "I know. Listen, I have to take the ride anyway. Don't slow it down for me, either. If I think it's okay, then we'll leave it as is."

"Okay. And thanks, Marianne." The crew chief turned to Doug as the next empty car slid into view. "You want to go with her?"

Doug glanced at Marianne, then nodded affirmatively.

They were strapped into the two-man space capsule, which was shaped something like a small canoe. Doug sat behind Marianne. She was strapped into the front seat, her spine and shoulders resting against his chest, her head tucked under his chin. His legs were on the outside of hers.

The car started moving slowly down the first long tunnel. Neon yellow and green lights led the way. For lack of a better place to put them, and since all hands were supposed to be kept inside the car, Doug wrapped his arms securely around her waist. "That okay?" he asked as the car made a grinding climb up the first incline.

Marianne nodded, already closing her eyes, her stomach feeling as if it had already dropped about fifteen inches. "That's fine." His arms made her feel safer, more secure.

The first sharp descent knocked the wind out of her. Nothing unusual. The car sped around the first curve, jolting them to the left, then down it went sharply, about twenty or thirty feet to the right. They were up again before Marianne could scream, winding around another curve, this time angling in hard to the right, then right again, and then unexpectedly left.

And so it continued, up, down, the screams of other riders reverberating through the dark cavernous caves. They sped past a space city on their left, and down again sharply past the winking neon lights of another space city, then back up again to the top where, seemingly, for a stretch of nearly thirty seconds they circled around and around at the top, their car suspended high and unprotected in the glittery darkness of a star-filled black velvet galaxy.

Doug's arms moved tighter around her as they hit the last curve and prepared for the final descent. They went down one curve and around another. Marianne sucked in her breath and prepared herself for the worst and steepest decline.

Only it never happened. Without warning, their car had slowed down, slid, then cranked and screeched to a stop. They were on an angle, forty-five degrees down, at the beginning of another tunnel. As her eyes adjusted, Marianne could make out the shadows of the roller-coaster track, and the black walls on either side of them.

"Is that part of the Space City experience, too?" Doug asked, his arms not loosening in the slightest.

Marianne leaned her head against his shoulder, glad she wasn't alone there, stranded in the dark. There were worse places to be stuck, she knew—at the top, for one—but right now her position felt scary enough.

"No." She sighed, trying to resign herself to what might be a very long wait. "More like a power outage or machine malfunction. Don't worry. We're safe enough. Each car has three separate sets of brakes and the track locks up automatically. But it may be several minutes before we get going again."

In the distance they could hear several screams. Someone yelling to get out of there—now. Someone else shouting reassurance. Teenage kids—laughing and crowing over their fortune.

Listening, Doug laughed softly. "I know what they mean. If I were a teenager on a date this is exactly where I'd want to get lost."

"Hard to neck strapped into a car," Marianne said wryly, before she could think.

"Oh, I don't know," Doug murmured, suddenly playful. His lips touched her hair, then moved lazily down her ear in a way that took Marianne's breath away. "I think the possibilities are endless."

Footsteps sounded behind them. Doug moved away from Marianne just as someone approached them and a flashlight was beamed in Marianne's face. "Ms. Spencer?"

"Yes."

"Sorry about this," the worker said matter of factly. "We're having a little trouble with a power outage. It's been kind of erratic all day. My boss heard you were here and he wants to talk to you. He's upstairs in the control room." He held out a hand.

Marianne unstrapped her belt, and with the maintenance man's help, climbed out of the car. She couldn't help but notice how sweaty he smelled, as if he hadn't bothered to use deodorant that day, or it had long ago worn off, and she moved back slightly. From then on she decided to keep an airy distance from him.

The maintenance man shined his flashlight at Doug. "Sir, if you'll just stay where you are, we'll have you all out of here in a jiffy."

Doug looked at Marianne. After a second's hesitation, she nodded. "If the car gets started before I return, I'll meet you downstairs at the exit, all right?"

"Okay," he said, smiling, "but the ride won't be the same without you."

Marianne followed the worker down a narrow ramp. Stairs led to a hallway. His light beaming the way in the darkness, they moved down several more passageways before finally coming to the control room. It, too, was dark.

The man ahead of her said nothing. She didn't expect a lot of conversation and didn't push it. Nonetheless the hairs on the back of her neck stood up. Marianne wondered briefly at her unease but decided it was due to the heights. Meandering down stairs, through passageways and tunnels, they were still a long way from the ground, and the continuing darkness, the thought of the ride breaking down merely compounded her fears.

She didn't like being on or around roller coasters to begin with. To be on one when it malfunctioned... well, it was understandable she would feel on edge. Especially with Doug still back there on the track.

They reached the control room, where the controls to the generator were located and the entire ride was monitored via videotape. Marianne stepped in, saw the television screens that depicted every inch of track. They were fine. It was the men sitting in front of the control panels that were in need of help. Both were slumped forward, their heads draped over their limp arms.

A scream started up in her throat but it was cut off by the door behind her being slammed shut.

Two other shadowy men in CWR uniforms stepped toward her.

Simultaneously, from behind her, she felt a prick in her arm. Something sharp, like a needle. Then a hand at her mouth cut off the choked cries of anguish. She'd never really learned to scream, Marianne thought, at least not well enough. And then, oh, God....

Just that quickly she couldn't seem to move. Or stand. Or even hold open her eyes.

Already falling, she was shoved into a chair, her limp body held back forcibly. She smelled sweat and cologne and male bodies. Nausea rose up in her throat as a blindfold was yanked unceremoniously over her eyes.

She tried to resist, but with her mind spinning, her body all but useless, there was little she could do. And as the seconds ticked past, there was little she wanted to do. She felt too woozy to struggle; she felt incredibly blissful, in fact, considering she was being held against her will.

Her mind and body spinning, she heard questions coming at her through the drug-induced fog. "What is the Navy's involvement at CWR? Why are they here?" a harsh unaccented voice demanded.

She meant to say nothing, but heard herself answering the clipped, peculiar voice. "What do you mean why are they here? Stan worked for the Navy. So does Joe..." She laughed, unable to understand their ignorance. "Stan is dead and Joe is missing, so of course the Navy is here."

They murmured between themselves impatiently. "Where is Joe?"

"Don't know. No one knows..." Without warning, she felt like she'd had a one-two punch, either that or a triple martini. Her tongue felt thick and clumsy. It was all she could do to stay upright in the chair, never mind think or breathe.

"Why is the FBI here?"

She was getting sleepier and sleepier; it was all she could do to stay awake. "To help," she said, struggling uselessly, limply, against the arms that held her.

"Help what?" They were shaking her rudely, another saying in a clipped, foreign-sounding tongue, "You fool! You have given her too much!"

They were shaking her again. "What does the FBI want? What do the local police suspect?" asked the man with the clipped, peculiar voice.

Suspect? "That Stan was murdered...."

They were leaning closer again, and everything was slipping away. Marianne struggled to stay upright, but she was slipping and falling like the oldest rag doll, tumbling right out of the chair. Her shoulder ached as she hit the floor. And then, blissfully, she fell head over heels into an endless black pit.

# Chapter Six

"I can't believe I just let you go off with him," Doug said, bending over Marianne in the first-aid station.

She felt tremendously hung over and put a trembling hand to her head. "Don't be ridiculous. He was in a CWR uniform. We were in the middle of a power outage. There's no way you could have known."

Doug scowled. He helped her sit up, then looked at the physician on call. "You're sure she's going to be all right?"

"She'll be fine," the doctor assured him. "But it may take another half an hour or so for those drugs to wear off." He turned to Marianne. "I suggest you just lie here and wait it out before you try to go home. Mr. Maitland, you may stay if you like. And, Marianne, we probably should call the Cypress City police. I don't know what this is all about but—"

"Later." She waved him off. "I'll do it when I get back to my office." She wasn't up to dealing with any of that now. And unfortunately, she knew what it was about: Doug's father. There were a couple of men, if memory served her correctly, who were very scared and worried. Obviously, Joe or Stan had stumbled onto something nefarious. And now the crooks were trying to get them before they were turned in.

The door shut. Doug came toward her, his shoulders blocking out everything else, and he sat down beside her on the cot. The antiseptic smells of the clinic surrounded them both.

"Maybe we should get you under the covers," Doug said, fussing over her like a mother hen.

She did feel like sleeping, but she also knew this was no time for her to rest, no matter how tempting sounded the idea of escaping the pressure and tension for just a little while. "I feel enough of an invalid as it is," she grumbled argumentatively, deciding that was her best excuse.

"Yeah, well—" He sighed and, taking her palm in his, rubbed her knuckles gently with his thumb. He'd been terrified when she hadn't come back, but by the time he'd decided to go and find her, the ride had started up again and Marianne had been found. He'd had to thread his way through a crowd of dissenting people to talk to the crew chief, who fortunately had remembered him. By then, the first-aid workers were arriving.

No one had seen the men who had done this to Marianne. In the darkness of the ride's interior, he hadn't gotten a look at the man's face. The men in the control room upstairs had been knocked out, too—but not by drugs, by fists. They, too, were recovering, in another room. So far, the park was behaving as if this were a routine matter. Doug knew it was fast turning into life or death. The men who were responsible for this—whoever they were—hadn't killed again, yet. They might decide to soon, particularly if they felt threatened.

They had to remember something, anything, that would be a clue to the men's identities. Maybe if he and Marianne went over it together... "You want to talk about it?" he asked, not wanting to push her when she obviously still felt so bad, but wanting to work out the details of what had gone on just the same.

Marianne was aware she was just beginning to be coherent again. And no, if truth be told, she really didn't want to talk about it. It was humiliating, the way she'd been duped. She took a deep breath. "Not really, but maybe I should."

"The guy who led you off. I didn't get a good look at his face. Did you?"

"No."

"You couldn't identify him?"

She shook her head negatively. "No, just that he was taller than me, a lean, wiry build. He smelled like sweat. He had that Children's World cap pulled down low over his brow."

"No distinguishing marks?"

"No. He was just the average clean-shaven worker, didn't even wear glasses, from what I could tell. Of course it wasn't really light until we got to the control room, and then I didn't look at him, either." Fool that she was, she'd been too busy thinking about Doug, and her growing feelings for him, wrapped up in remembering what a pleasurable experience the heretofore frightening ride had been when she'd ridden with him, his strong arms wrapped securely around her.

She looked up into his face and realized he knew she'd been drifting off—somewhat sappily—into daydreams. He looked amused. She felt herself begin to blush.

Doug grinned. "What you just said, about thinking about me," he prompted.

She was shocked, and a little disbelieving. "I—I said that out loud?"

"Yeah. Although it was kind of mumbled. You still must be feeling the effects of that drug they gave you."

"Must be." She clamped her lips shut and refused to say anything else.

He watched her again, and alert to the reason for her wariness, smiled some more.

"It's all right," he said softly. "I already know how you feel anyway."

"You can't—" she started to argue.

"It's written all over your face every time you look at me," he contradicted softly.

She knew it was. She could hardly stay away from him, and she couldn't ever seem to stop thinking about him. And if she were honest with herself, she knew it was a lot more than the stress and the tension of the situation bringing them together. It was a basic chemistry. It was the protected yet vulnerable way she'd felt when he was holding her in his arms. It was the way he was looking at her now. They pushed all the wrong buttons in each other, and they pushed all the right ones, too.

"But this fascination we're feeling right now is neither here nor there at the moment," he said gently, seeking to reassure her, to let her know he wouldn't rush her again. "We'll deal with that later. When you're more ready to accept it. Right now I need to know why they drugged you, what they hoped to accomplish. You said they asked you some questions."

"I did?"

"Yeah. When they first brought you in here. You said they were talking about Stan and my dad."

Marianne closed her eyes, trying to remember. And then it came to her. "They think Joe's alive," she said slowly, aware she was still a little groggy and disoriented. "They're worried about him."

"Worried? Why?"

"I don't know. Just that he poses some sort of a threat to them."

"Can you remember anything else?"

"One of the men spoke with a heavy foreign accent. German or Russian, something like that. I'm no expert."

Doug was silent. It was her turn for questions. "What do you know about what happened over there?"

His look turned grim. "The power outage was deliberate. A couple of the guards were knocked out."

"How?"

"We don't know. Either someone on the complex here is helping them, or we've got a couple of thugs who are pros at getting in and out of sticky places. Whatever it is, it was obvious they wanted you."

"What about the phone call to my office?"

"It was a setup. Several people did get sick on the ride today, though. Probably the heat. But no one at Space City called for you to come over and check it out. Nor were they asked to." Doug drew a hand through his hair in a frustrated gesture. "I think this has something to do with my dad. With his reason for being here, with the reason the Navy wants him, too. I might as well tell you, Commander Keel and Bryant Rockwell are both on their way over here. They want to talk to you."

Marianne smiled wanly. "Great." She didn't relish being in another Navy-FBI battle over jurisdiction.

Although Commander Keel and Bryant went over and over the afternoon's episode with her, Marianne failed to remember anything else. Both men eventually left frustrated. Once the drug wore off and Marianne felt better, she headed back to the office.

Doug was worried about her, and he went with her, just to make sure she was all right. As it happened, she was glad he had, because when she got back to her office among her messages was a very important discovery.

Maids at the Gay Nineties hotel had found a room full of mysterious belongings. The man who'd checked in, Franklin Koslovsky, had never returned. Not even to sleep. The reservations clerk had checked the address Mr. Koslovsky had given and found it to be an empty lot in St. Louis. Now his reservation was up and they didn't know what to do.

"I'll be right over to have his things put in storage," Marianne said. As per CWR policy, the belongings would be held until restitution was made on his bill. If it ever was.

She hung up. Doug knew from the look on her face something was up. Briefly she explained.

"You think it might be Stan's room?"

"I think there's a chance. I was wondering if it might belong to one of the thugs that seems to be running around here, knocking people out. In any case, I'll find out when we get there."

"Does this sort of thing happen very often?" Doug asked, falling into step beside her.

"Practically never."

"Mind if I tag along?"

She didn't seem to have much choice, although she was beginning to like having him along. "You know this is highly irregular," she cautioned as they reached her car.

"So is having your father missing."

They arrived at the Gay Nineties hotel in record time. A sprawling white building that housed some nine hundred rooms, it was situated on Bay Lake, three miles down from Doug's hotel. Koslovsky's room was on the ninth floor. Marianne entered via a passkey, her heart pumping at double speed.

At first glance, it looked like a normal tourist room. There were two closed suitcases on the bureau, and a video camera and case. She began to relax, as did Doug. Taking the lead, he examined the camera, while she looked through the clothes draped over an armchair. Finding nothing that would help them, she turned to Doug.

"Find anything?" she asked.

Doug shook his head as he rummaged through the case. "No. But there are several unopened rolls of thirty-five millimeter film. They've still got the cellophane and price tags on them. They were bought at a gift shop here in Children's World."

"Is there a name on the camera case?" Marianne asked, moving to join him.

Doug shook his head. While Marianne searched the bureaus, he walked around. In the corner of the closet was a battered guitar case, covered with stickers. Doug's face lit up with recognition, then it turned very pale. "This belonged to Stan," he said in a thickened voice.

"Did he have a habit of registering in hotels under an alias?" she asked.

Doug gave his head a negative shake, still looking at the guitar case. He opened it up and lovingly ran his hands over the strings. "No. He must have been working on a case—probably with Dad. That's the only explanation."

"So we did find his room." Marianne tried the suitcases but found them both locked. She sighed her frustration. "Got a bobby pin?"

"No. Sorry. Don't normally carry them."

"Neither do I. I'll be right back." She slipped out of the room and came back several moments later, a pin and a small metal nail file in hand. "In case the other doesn't work."

It took them almost a half an hour, but they finally pried the suitcases open. In one was simply clothes. In another, they hit the jackpot. They found a five-by-seven-inch notebook full of numbers and letters that were obviously some kind of code. Unfortunately, there was no key in the book that would allow them to decipher what they had found. Nonetheless, Doug was elated, and Marianne shared his feelings of success. "This is it, positive proof he was working on a case," Doug said victoriously, studying what looked to be lines and lines of gibberish.

"And planning to do a heck of a lot of guitar playing as well," Marianne said, indicating the stack of old marked-up music.

Doug shrugged off the music. "Oh. He and Dad had a jam session every time they got together."

"It was normal for Stan to bring this much music?"

"Oh, yeah. He toted that everywhere he took his guitar. Do you think we should hand this over to the FBI?"

Stan had been Navy, though. And if it were code...
"Why not Commander Keel?" Marianne asked.

Doug frowned. "I don't trust him."

Marianne sighed her relief, glad he shared her emotions. "Neither do I. Whenever I'm around him I'm never sure which side he's on."

"But you know he's looking out for number one." Marianne nodded. "Whereas Bryant is Seth's friend." In Doug's mind that apparently made him someone they could trust.

Marianne knew Bryant had bent over backward to aid the family; yet she had her reservations about involving him. "He's also a government employee, Doug. It'd be unethical, at the very least, for him to know about this and not share it with Keel. I'm not sure we should put him in that position. It's really not fair."

"And if there's a leak in Keel's department?"

"What other explanation is there for him not knowing what Joe and Stan were doing here? Unless Joe and Stan didn't trust him to know."

"Or unless Keel himself is the bad guy. If he is, that certainly explains why he came down here alone, and is not using his own men for backup." Instead, Marianne thought, Keel was doing the investigating himself, filtering the information he thought suitable back to his colleagues in Washington by phone. Sure, there were a couple of Navy men around from the base, but they were more or less bodyguards for Keel, or lackeys. Neither seemed to have any real authority or experience.

Doug continued, "Maybe we should keep this to ourselves, at least until my dad is found."

"When he does come in, we can give it to him," Marianne said confidently. For Doug's sake, for everyone's, she had to believe Joe was still alive. "He'll know what to do."

"So where do we put it in the meantime?" Doug asked.

Since his room had already been trashed, they couldn't put anything there. "We can stash Stan's personal belongings in my apartment for safekeeping," Marianne decided.

"Fine, but I think I'll keep the notebook with me."

"You're sure?" It was a risk keeping it, a risk putting it anywhere else.

"I want to give a copy of it to Billy. Hell, I'll make several copies, mail them here and there. I've got some friends I can trust to hang on to something for me for a couple of days."

"That's probably a pretty good idea."

"Yeah. I'll tell them if anything happens to me to turn it over to the family, and if that's not possible, then my attorney." He tapped the notebook against his palm. "It's essential whatever was in here not be destroyed."

Marianne knew his idea made sense, yet she was on edge, too. "If this is the reason Stan was killed—"

"And there's reason to think that's so."

"It could be dangerous for Billy to have it."

"Don't forget, he's Navy. He can take care of himself. He's also a communications specialist. And a damn fine one at that. If anyone can break the code . . ."

Marianne knew that if Doug had confidence in his brother, it was well founded. And though her dispensing of "Mr. Koslovski's" property this way was strictly against all regulations, she was willing to take the risk and make an exception in this case. Especially if it helped Doug's father come back or stay alive. "All right," she said. Maybe there was something in the notebook that, if decoded, would help them find Joe. And at this point they needed every single bit of help they could get.

"WHERE IN HELL COULD THE FOOL have put it?" the swarthy man grumbled irritably, weaving in and out among the tourists in the Enchanted Village late Thursday evening. The park would close in another couple of hours, and they were no closer to finding their lost valuables than they had been days ago, when the travesty had first occurred. Hoping it would help, he once again reviewed the facts he and his compatriot knew. "He had it with him when he left Liberty Hall."

"He had it when he boarded the monorail from the International Bazaar to here." The thin man struck his fist against the palm of his other hand. More difficult for him than acting the tourist was keeping his voice unaccented, and peppered with American slang. He did not want to stand out. Not in a crowd, not anywhere. Fortunately, there were so many visitors from other parts of the world at Children's World, it didn't really matter if he became tense and lapsed slightly and inadvertently used his homeland accent.

"But he didn't have it when we caught up with him the next day." The swarthy man continued to stare at his surroundings. There was the Twelve Dancing Princesses Ride nearby, dark and cozy. There were many places to dump the information, including the water rides, which featured pirates, dark caves and treasure chests.

"Maybe he ditched it in the 20,000 Leagues lagoon. Maybe that's why he jumped the fence."

"Do not be foolish. He jumped the fence to get away from us. Though perhaps if we'd had more time—"

"Do not delude yourself. He would not have talked, not without . . . torture."

"Perhaps. And perhaps not. It does not matter now."

"You are right. Even with the serum, he was resistant."

"Our only hope is to find it," the other said, discouraged, sweating, afraid. "We cannot go back without it. Not after—"

"The mistake."

They were quiet again.

The two men looked at one another, recognition dawning. "What about the obvious?" asked the thin man.

"Yes. Why not?" They only hoped it wasn't already gone.

"WHAT DO YOU MEAN all the gift shops in the Enchanted Village were broken into overnight?" Marianne demanded first thing Friday morning. "What about the alarm systems? The security guards?"

"The guards were knocked out," her boss said. "The alarm systems disconnected. Face it, Marianne. We're dealing with pros here. And I don't like it one bit."

"What did they take?"

Nina sighed. "Now comes the odd part. Nothing, apparently."

Marianne stared at her. She felt as if she were still in the middle of a bad dream. "You're kidding."

"No." Nina paused and shook her head as if that would clear it. "I only wish I was. But get this." She gave Marianne a beleaguered look and lit a cigarette. "There was something weird. All the Wacky Duck dolls were cut open."

"Why, for God's sake?"

"You tell me. It could have been a teenage prank. Or maybe it's an indication we have something more disturbing going on here." Nina gave her another hard look, as if she were trying to read Marianne's mind. "A smuggling operation, for instance."

"You can't be serious."

"Those dolls come from Japan. If someone wanted to get something into the country without customs knowing—"

"What better cover than inside a Wacky Duck doll," Marianne finished the thought. "What do you think it is? Jewelry? Electronics?"

"I don't know. That's what I'd like you to find out."

*Why not just assign me to go to the moon?* Marianne thought sarcastically. But she could see Nina was serious. And also very worried. "I'll get right on it," she said solemnly, planning to immediately go over to the shops to view the damage. She had to face it. This wasn't a bad dream, but reality.

Nina blew out the smoke she'd been holding in her lungs. "Before you go, how are the Maitlands holding up?"

"About as well as can be expected," Marianne said cautiously, turning back to her boss. Why the sudden interest? "They're worried, of course."

"Of course."

"But fairly calm anyway."

"I see." Nina paused. "Have they seen much of the park since they've been here?"

Now that was a strange question. If there was one thing Nina avoided dealing with, it was other people's private lives. She liked numbers and ledgers and facts. Nothing that touched the soul. "Well, no, they haven't."

Nina put her cigarette down and reached for her calendar. Perusing the page for that day, she suggested mildly, "I think under the circumstances they could use a night out. Why not arrange a special dinner for them? Perhaps a table at the Seven Seas luau? They'd enjoy that."

"I'm sure they would," Marianne said. If she could get them there, that was. Doug had taken the notebook over to Billy for decoding. She hadn't seen or heard from him since, though she knew he had played another gig at the Starlight Lounge the previous evening. It had taken all she had to stay away from the lounge, but she'd known she had to. She liked him. But she couldn't risk getting any more personally involved with him than she already was; the potential for hurt was too great, and she had already been hurt enough.

Nina looked up and took another drag on her cigarette. "And, Marianne, you be there, too. Just to make sure everything goes smoothly. When this is all over, however it turns out, I want them to be left with the impression the CWR people did everything possible to make this crisis situation easier."

"Certainly." She forced a smile. Suddenly her boss was watching her every move. If this blew up in their faces, both their jobs could be on the line.

The dinner tonight had to run smoothly; it had to.

"THAT WAS MARIANNE ON THE PHONE just now." Doug stalked across Billy's hotel room Friday morning, and moved onto the balcony, where his brother had been sitting, the morning paper folded open on his lap, for the better part of a half hour. "CWR wants to treat us to a dinner tonight. The luau. You up for it?"

Billy stared listlessly at the paper. "Sure. Why not?" he said finally.

Doug knew his brother had been worried about their father. Of all the Maitlands, he had taken it the hardest. But maybe that was because Billy was alone. Pam had Seth, after all, and he had Marianne ready to lend an ear whenever he needed to talk about what was happening. Only Billy had no one close of the opposite sex to confide in. But that's the way Billy had always preferred it—alone. Doug wondered if he was regretting that now.

"You okay?" Doug asked.

"Yeah." But Billy remained silent for several more moments. Finally, realizing Doug deserved some sort of explanation, he handed his older brother the front page. "There was another reconnaissance plane shot down in the Gulf last night."

Doug scanned the article, then looked at Billy. Clearly, this hit him hard; those ships were his home, the crewmen and pilots his buddies. "Anyone you knew?" he asked gently, wishing there was something more he could do or say.

"No. But it's the third in six months. It shouldn't be happening, Doug. We go to incredible lengths to keep our codes secret."

Doug could see his brother's frustration was acute. But he also knew there was nothing Billy could do, now, anyway, for the men who had died. He could, however, help their dad.

"About that notebook I gave you," he said softly. So far, it was just between the two men, and Marianne, of course. Neither had told Pam or Seth about finding Stan's room. Pam and Seth had both brought work with them from D.C. and lately Pam hadn't looked good and Seth was still nursing his injured hand. Doug didn't want them feeling any more pressure or tension than they already were. "Have you had any luck?"

Billy shook his head and swore colorfully, letting Doug know just how hard he'd tried. "And I was up most of the night wrestling with it, too. It's like no code I've ever seen. I don't have any idea what it is."

Doug had expected his brother to have success within hours. In retrospect, he could see he'd been naive. "Can't you break it?"

"No. I need a computer. I called Marianne. She's getting me a terminal, on loan."

Doug had been busy, too. During the night he'd painstakingly made four copies of the code, one for Bill to study, three to send to his friends around the country. The original had been hidden in his trumpet case, between a hole he'd carved in the velvet cover and the hard case. It hadn't been hard to do. He'd had another gig at the Starlight Lounge. He'd taken the notebook over to the Vista Hotel, and then between sets made the transfer in his dressing room, behind a locked door. Later, after he'd finished playing, his trumpet had been locked up with all the other instruments in the lounge's vault for safekeeping. Doug felt a sense of satisfaction, knowing the notebook was secure, that no one else, not even his brother, knew where the original was. It wasn't that he didn't trust them, but that he felt they might be in danger knowing. This secret was all his.

At least until his father came back.

Doug noticed his brother was looking at him strangely. Doug knew he'd been daydreaming, but he'd been doing that a lot lately. When he wasn't thinking about his dad, puzzling over Joe's disappearance and Stan's death, he was thinking about Marianne.

She hadn't come to his gig, though he'd half expected her to. He'd been disappointed when she hadn't shown up. But kiss or no kiss, he was still the type of man she did not want to get involved with.

"I'm sure the computer will help," he encouraged his brother when it seemed some cheerleading was needed.

Billy sighed, none the happier. "I still have to break the code, Doug." His outlook was dismal, and he described it with several salty phrases. "It could take days."

"But you will do it." Doug was counting on his brother to come through. So, probably, was his dad.

"Yeah, I'll get it," Billy said determinedly. He passed a hand over his military haircut, and then looked back at Doug, the fear in his eyes raw and tangible—something Doug felt every waking moment and tried just as hard to deny.

"I only hope it's not too late."

## Chapter Seven

Seven o'clock rolled around, and then eight, and still Marianne was stuck in her office, her mind whirling with questions and fears and unanswered puzzles. Where was Doug's father? He'd been gone five days now. Why hadn't he called anyone in the family that clearly loved him so much? Was Joe safe as they all hoped or was he dead like Stan Howell? And what had the two men been secretly investigating at Children's World? Was the answer in the notebook they had found? And what had the video camera been for? Was there a smuggling ring at Children's World? It seemed almost too incredible to imagine anything being smuggled in Wacky Duck dolls. But then, she'd never expected anyone to administer truth serum to her, either. Even knowing they hadn't intended to kill her didn't alleviate her tension. She felt as if they were all in constant danger, as if one wrong step would land them all in the sort of Dantesque hell she'd only read about in books or seen on movie screens.

"Hadn't you better get home to change?" Nina Granger stopped in the doorway to Marianne's office, briefcase in hand. "Or are you going to the luau as is?"

"I'm out of here."

"See you in the morning." Nina strode off down the hall toward the elevators.

Marianne followed minutes later.

She knew something was wrong the moment she unlocked the door to her apartment. For one thing, her hall closet was standing open.

A scream in her throat, she started to back toward the hall. But on the second step she encountered a body; simultaneously, two leather-gloved hands were clamped over her eyes and her mouth. She felt a terrifying déjà vu.

Her accoster kicked the door shut behind them. Struggling furiously, Marianne flailed and screamed, but little sound escaped past the hand clamped around her mouth. She heard the man swear. Kicking her foot back, she dug the pointed end of her heel into his foot.

He swore again and tightened the hand on her mouth brutally, making her gasp in pain. The next thing she knew she was falling face down on the floor, her captor's body slamming down violently over hers.

The breath was knocked out of her. She felt like one raw, giant scrape. She tried weakly to turn, to crawl away, to scream for help, but there was still no air in her lungs. Then a blow landed on her neck.

This time Marianne did groan. She felt the pain, like a giant wave of agony to her brain. And then nothing at all as she slipped into a great black void.

When she came to, her hands and feet were tied behind her and roped together. There was a gag over her mouth that cut into her chin and sucked all the moisture out of her mouth. Her neck was aching; her arms and legs were numb. Glancing around her, she saw the apartment was still dark. And, apparently, empty.

A sigh of relief rippled through her, followed swiftly by feelings of rage and indignation. She wiggled around on her belly, feeling like a fish who'd been hauled up out of water and dropped on the shore. She was helpless, completely out of her element. Dammit all, how was she going to get free?

"MARIANNE?" DOUG SHOUTED, knocking on her front door, more than a little annoyed she hadn't shown up for dinner as scheduled. "Marianne, are you in there?"

There were several sounds from inside the apartment, but no verbal reply. Something was wrong. Acting purely on instinct, Doug put a shoulder to the door, rammed against it and forced it open. He found Marianne on the floor. She was bound with a phone cord and gagged with a scarf. Kneeling beside her, he loosened the bonds, then pulled off the gag.

Tears of relief were streaming down her face. He pulled her up into his lap and stroked her hair. His heart was beating as rapidly as if he'd just finished a ten-mile race. "God, Marianne, what happened? Who did this to you?"

"I don't know." She took a deep breath and brushed the tears away with the back of her hand. "I didn't get a good look at him. He was here in my apartment when I got home."

"Did he hurt you?" he asked angrily, aware for the first time how scared he had been, and how relieved and furious he was now.

She was shaking like a leaf in the wind. "Not really. He knocked me out for a while, I guess, but I'm okay now." She let out a shuddering breath and the tears started again.

He held her closer still while the emotional storm passed. When she had calmed down enough, they started from the beginning. She told him about coming home and finding her closet door open, then having someone come up behind her. It had been dark, she hadn't got a good look at his face, but she felt he might have been wearing a ski mask. He'd been of medium height, strong, medium weight. He'd had on gloves.

"Did he speak?" Doug asked. Now that her tears had stopped and she'd recovered, he had no real reason to keep holding her close. He also knew he didn't want to stop, and that it would take a heartfelt demand from her to prompt her release.

But this once she didn't try to move away. She huddled close against him, the damp side of her face pressed into his shoulder. "Not a word. He just grabbed me and shoved a gloved hand over my mouth."

"So there'll be no fingerprints." Doug lapsed into a frustrated silence. This whole ordeal was getting stranger all the time. "You're absolutely sure it was a man? Not a teenager or maybe a woman?"

Marianne closed her eyes and thought a moment. "Yes," she said after a moment. "It was definitely a man. He was taller than me, and strong. Big hands. A big frame."

"Anything else?"

"He wore a lot of after-shave, a cloying, musky scent. I didn't like it. It was too overpowering."

Well, there at least was something they could go on, Doug thought, feeling her shudder. "Could you identify the scent if you smelled it again?"

"Maybe. Probably." She paused and moved far enough away from him so she could see his face. "What do you think he was after?'' Now that the terror had passed, her curiosity had reasserted itself tenfold.

"I don't know." Doug shrugged. "Stan's belongings maybe." That was the obvious target. Had someone discovered they'd found his room? "Where did you put them?"

It was Marianne's turn to swear in frustration. "All over the place. Under my bed. In the closet. In the piano bench."

They looked in the closet. To her relief, Stan's camera was there. His suitcases filled with clothes were under her bed. His guitar was in her guest-room closet. The huge stack of music he'd left was in the piano bench. "Everything's here?" Doug asked.

Marianne nodded. "I must've got here before they had time to take anything."

"Maybe," Doug speculated. "But then maybe they had already got what they wanted before you arrived. Think about it. If you were knocked out, they could've taken anything they wanted. They could have torn the place apart."

"Like they did your hotel rooms," Marianne said slowly. But they hadn't. And that meant what? That they weren't looking for anything but her? But that didn't make any sense.

Before they could say anything more, there was a knock at the door. Bryant and Billy came rushing in, followed closely by Pam and Seth. "We were worried when you didn't show up," Billy said, after Doug had explained what had transpired.

"Do you think it was the same person who broke into our rooms?" Pam asked Bryant. Without warning, she looked as pale and shaken as Marianne.

Bryant, who'd been looking around, scowling and thinking, shook his head. He stalked back and forth, searching under paintings, underneath lamps. "I don't think it was the same person," he said quietly but firmly. Turning around, he faced them all, "For starters, the m.o. is too different. Whoever was here tonight wasn't a slasher."

"So then what did he want?" Marianne asked.

"Maybe he wanted to plant something," Bryant said.

"Like what? A listening device?"

"Stranger things have happened." Bryant cast a look at Billy. "Help me look around, will you?"

For the next fifteen minutes they looked under and over everything in her apartment. The search turned up nothing. "Well," Bryant said with a sigh when he'd finished checking her phone, "the place appears to be clean."

"You going to call the Cypress City police?" Billy asked, his tone sympathetic, as he moved to stand next to Marianne.

She shook her head after a moment's hesitation. "No. I—nothing's missing. I can't identify the guy. It would only be a bureaucratic mess." She didn't want the police there interviewing everyone, and she certainly didn't want the press.

Bryant paused, seeming to disagree. "Look, I understand this would be hard for you, but—"

"No arguments," Doug said calmly. He supported Marianne's decision; she'd already been through enough. "I think Marianne's right," he said quietly. "It has been a long night. And I really don't think the police could be much help at this point."

Bryant glanced at Marianne again. He seemed not to want to leave. Doug watched jealously as Bryant walked over to take Marianne's hand in his own. "If there's anything I can do, any way you think the FBI might be of service—"

"I'll call."

"Good. 'Cause I'll help you in any way I can. I just have one question to ask."

Marianne regarded him warily.

"Is there any way—Do you think your accoster could have been Joe Maitland?"

She sighed. So he was thinking and wondering that, too.

"WILL YOU RELAX? He didn't mean it," Marianne said to Doug half an hour later, after everyone else had left. She'd never seen Doug looking so angry or tense, not even that first day in her office.

"Yeah, he did. He thinks my dad is up to no good."

Marianne couldn't dispute that. Bryant had been nice, but suspicious. Not just of Joe, but of everything. But then that was what he was trained to do. "Well, can you blame him?" she said finally, searching for a way to calm Doug down. "The circumstances are pretty damning, and who knows what Keel has been filling Bryant's ear with. Besides, maybe Bryant's right. Maybe it's not so farfetched. We do have Stan's belongings stashed here. We do have access to the notebook."

"Yeah, but Bryant doesn't know that."

"So? He can still put two and two together. Whoever was here tonight didn't slash anything. He didn't tear anything up, or plant a listening device. He was probably looking for something specific—"

"You think it was my dad, too?"

"I don't know. I'm saying he could have been. Your dad is a big guy, right? Almost six feel tall? Strong? In good shape?"

"He doesn't wear horrible-smelling after-shave."

Marianne was quiet. "Well, maybe it wasn't after-shave I smelled, but his clothes. Or—"

"Did your accoster smell unwashed?"

She saw Doug's point. If his father had been on the lam, he may not have had time or opportunity to bathe or change his clothes.

She was silent a moment, remembering the scent of her accoster, the strong underlying scent of pine—and musk. "No, it wasn't that, it was after-shave."

Doug swore and stopped prowling long enough to sit down. Silence descended on them. Marianne sighed and shut her eyes. She put a hand to her forehead, aware they weren't getting anywhere. Were they dumb, blind, or just amateurs way out of their depth?

"Do you have a headache?"

"The worst," she admitted. She was also frightened. For herself. For Doug. His father. What were they up against?

"I'll get you some aspirin. Where is it?"

"In the kitchen. The cabinet above the stove."

She followed him into the kitchen. Intending to fix them both a soda, she got down two glasses and filled them with ice. But suddenly her hands were shaking so she couldn't get the cap off the bottle of soda. She knew it was a delayed reaction to all that had happened, but she couldn't seem to control her quaking fingers.

"Here, let me." Doug took it from her and poured.

Aware he was watching her every movement, Marianne dutifully swallowed the aspirin.

"Better?"

She nodded slowly. She was beginning to feel a little too fussed over. The urge to just throw herself into his safe, strong arms was beginning to overwhelm her. If he kept looking at her like that—so tenderly—she wasn't sure she would be able to fight it.

She took a sip of the soda.

Suddenly Doug was restless. "Mind if I have another look around?" he asked abruptly.

"Be my guest." This once she wanted him peeking in corners, making sure nothing was amiss.

He ended up concentrating on the hall closet and stood in front of it bewilderedly, shaking his head. Marianne followed him into the living room and settled on the sofa, kicking off her shoes and drawing her legs up under her. Amused by the half distasteful look on his face, Marianne looked past him, trying to see what he saw and not what she habitually ignored. Shoe boxes were stacked on top of a sweeper. There were boxes of Christmas decorations, several jackets, umbrellas, board games, a hat box and an antique milk jug. Not to mention the stacks of old magazines and two cases of canned Coke.

"I don't know," she said, walking over to him. "I think it has charm."

He slanted her a narrow glance that was teasing and warm. "It's disorganized as hell."

She grinned. "I like it that way."

He fought hard to keep the laughter out of his eyes and lost. "Why?"

She shrugged. "Maybe because the rest of the place is so ordered."

"It is, isn't it?" As naturally as if he did it every day, he laced an arm around her waist. She leaned into him briefly, liking the way his arm felt wrapped around her.

He was a man she could count on in a crisis; she was glad he was there for her.

Cautiously, he turned her toward him and slid a hand beneath her chin. Whatever Marianne had been about to say fled. She was left with impressions—the warmth of the man beside her, the strength.

"How about you?" he asked gently. At his closeness, an ache started deep inside her and spread outward in mesmerizing waves. "Are you perfectly organized and sublime, like the rest of your apartment?" He reached up to smooth the silky ends of her hair. When he finished his palm rested against the curve of her chin. "Or are you jumbled and wild and anything goes like that closet?"

"I don't know," she said quietly, as his thumb gently stroked her cheek. Part of her was prim, and yet deeper she was wild, untamed, free. Being around Doug made her want to feel that way more often.

"Marianne," he whispered. And then he did what he'd been wanting to all night. He kissed her. Once he'd started, he couldn't seem to stop. He inhaled sharply, hugged her tight and kissed her again. For the first time she felt the depth of his need and knew it matched her own. She felt his tenderness—it was there in the brush of his lips against hers, the subtle ever-changing pressure of his mouth, the alternately light and voracious sweep of his tongue.

He drew away from her slowly. His eyes were serious as he said, "I don't want you to be alone tonight."

Marianne didn't want that, either.

"I'll sleep on the sofa," he promised quietly, reading the sudden wariness in her eyes. "Kind of like an on-premises security guard."

Marianne grinned, glad he was able to lightly gloss over the attraction between them. She didn't know what the future held for them; she wasn't ready to put it to the test. For the moment, they had enough to deal with.

## Chapter Eight

Doug awakened to the smell of frying bacon and freshly brewed coffee. When he joined Marianne in the kitchen minutes later, her hair was still damp from the shower. She was wearing makeup, but it couldn't hide the paleness of her skin or the violet shadows beneath her eyes. He found himself wishing he could erase them. "Aren't you going in to work today?" he asked.

"Saturday's my day off. I had thought about going in anyway, considering all that's been going on, but after what happened last night, I decided to take time off."

He nodded, aware she'd never looked more beautiful or vulnerable—or unhappy in a quiet way. Was she ashamed of the vulnerability she'd shown him? The passion? Or just regretting a little of everything, starting with ever becoming involved with him and his family. If she did, well…he couldn't say he blamed her. Her life had been nothing but hell since he'd shown up.

She seemed to read his thoughts. Forcing a smile that was a little too cheerful, she said, "Help yourself to some coffee and have a seat."

For several minutes he watched her move back and forth. She was a natural in the kitchen, obviously as good a cook as she was an executive. "I guess I wasn't much of a protector," he said sheepishly. "I didn't even hear you come into the kitchen this morning."

"I know." She turned toward him and briefly her eyes glimmered with mischief, making him wonder just how long she had watched him sleep. Then she sobered. "But you were also up half the night. I heard you walking around."

"You didn't sleep well, either?" He already knew the answer, but he wanted to hear her say it. He wanted her to confide in him.

"I couldn't. Not knowing someone had been here." She shuddered involuntarily, keeping her eyes deliberately averted. She paused to remove the last of the bacon from the pan, for a moment giving that all her attention. "I felt violated." She set her spatula carefully on a ceramic spoon rest and turned to face him, her face ashen again.

It was all he could do not to get up and take her into his arms. "Yeah, I know," he said quietly. Doug had felt violated, too. And angry that he'd put Marianne in any kind of danger, however inadvertently. For her sake, though, he tried to look on the bright side. "At least they didn't trash your place."

"Yeah, I'm lucky there."

She slid his bacon and eggs onto a plate and brought them over to the table. She joined him seconds later. They ate in companionable silence.

"Anyway, thanks for staying last night," she said, picking up her fork.

He gave her a level look, knowing he shouldn't say what was on his mind, but doing it anyway. "It bothers you I was here, doesn't it?"

After a moment, she nodded. "Yeah. When I woke up this morning, I felt stupid, embarrassed over the way I behaved last night. I mean, I was such a fool. I've lived alone for the past fourteen years. It's not as if—"

"Wait a minute." He cut her off abruptly, feeling himself begin to get angry again. "Are we talking about you breaking down and crying—which I felt you had every justification in doing after what you'd been through."

She looked up fiercely. "I never cry."

"Never?"

"Well . . . almost never." Slight traces of pink crept into her cheeks.

"Doesn't that tell you something?"

"What? That I'm happy."

He got up and walked to her side. "That you've closed off your feelings too much."

"Doug." She got up, circling away from him, opening the doors that led out onto her small terrace.

He refused to let her off the hook that easily. "I'm not being critical. I'm being honest. You kissed me last night like—"

"Like a woman who'd had her apartment broken into."

"No. Like a woman who needed love. How long has it been since you've let someone be close to you, Marianne, really close?"

She couldn't, wouldn't answer. She turned away from him and stared at the lake.

In the morning sunlight, her hair glimmered a rich dark red. He reached up to touch the damp strands, pushing an errant lock away from her face. "There's no shame in wanting to be with someone, Marianne," he said softly. "No shame in needing."

"I've seen what allowing yourself to be emotionally dependent on another person does to a woman, Doug. It was my mother's fatal weakness. If she hadn't had my stepfather to go to, she would have stayed with my real father forever, never mind the fact his life-style was making all three of us miserable! But she just couldn't bear to be alone, and she told me so many, many times."

"And you're not going to let that happen to you."

She tossed her head proudly. "I've trained myself to be independent, self-supporting, self-reliant. I've built my own security." She seemed to feel his mere presence in her life threatened everything she had, and maybe it did, he mused thoughtfully. Because when he was with her, he felt increasingly that free choice was a thing of the past, like he had to be with her, had to know she was safe.

"Don't get me wrong. I applaud your ability to do just that." His hands were gentle on her shoulders as he made her face him. "But I can't help but wonder if maybe you haven't gone too far."

Her jaw tilted up another notch. "Because I don't have a man in my life?" she said curtly.

He shook his head and said softly, "Because you're lonely, as lonely as I am."

BILLY LOOKED UP from the computer as Doug walked into his hotel room. "Bryant stopped by. He's spending the day in the Enchanted Village, interviewing every possible worker or security person who might have seen Stan before his death."

Well, that was more than the Cypress City police were doing, Doug thought. "Any luck so far?"

Billy shook his head. "Bryant is damn frustrated, too. Seems all he can get from the concession and ride workers is the feeling that if you've seen one tourist, you've seen them all."

"Can't blame them, when they've got thousands streaming into the park daily."

"Yeah, I know what you mean." Billy typed in a few more possibilities and frowned at what resulted on the computer screen. "No one has seen anything weird, either."

"That's hard to believe isn't it?" Doug mused. "Considering the man was injected with truth serum shortly before he died."

"Maybe they did it in some rest-room stall. Or—or behind some bushes."

"Maybe."

Billy typed away. "Anyway, what are you going to do?"

"Take a shower. Go back and talk to Marianne. Maybe we can find out something on our own." He couldn't just sit around and do nothing. His father would expect more than that of him. And if anyone had CWR connections, Marianne did.

Billy slanted his older brother a knowing grin. Sensing his brother's hands-off mood, he sobered abruptly. "You really care about her, don't you?"

Yes, Doug thought, he did. He just couldn't be sure the feeling was returned.

WHEN DOUG RETURNED to Marianne's apartment an hour later, the most godawful discordant racket was floating out underneath her front door. Either she was the most unmusical person in this world, he thought, or there was something wrong with her piano, her hearing or both.

Almost afraid of what he'd find on the other side of the door, he rang the bell. Marianne answered the door, excited, her red hair flying out around her face. She grabbed him by the wrist and pulled him into her apartment, slamming the door behind him. "Wait till you see what I have to show you!" She dragged him over to the piano bench and patted a place on one end. "Have a seat."

"Are you sure—"

"Sh!" she hissed commandingly, hands poised over the keyboard. Then she began to play. "Isn't that great?" she crowed when she'd finished.

"I hate to tell you this, but that arrangement sounds nothing like 'Silk Stockings.'"

Her eyes glimmered with unchecked excitement. "I know," she said. "Doug, we've got it. The clue we've been looking for. It's here! In this music!"

Doug stared at the music numbly. Had he been blind? "The chords." Slowly, it dawned on him what she was saying. "How did you figure it out? How'd you know where to look?"

"Well, I didn't. I mean, I was going crazy trying to figure out what that guy could have been looking for in here last night, and finally it occurred to me if it was something of Stan's, and nothing had been taken, then it had to still be here, only we had obviously overlooked it, too. So I got everything out and went through it one more time. There was nothing in the guitar case or the clothes or the suitcases. Finally, it came down to this. I started playing it and...voilà. Do you think your brother could decode this?"

Doug frowned at the chords, which, although written out note by note on the staffs, had not been identified by letter and number name. "I doubt it. He doesn't read music. Is all the music like this?"

"No, that's the crazy thing. It was just this one, the photocopy of 'Silk Stockings,' that was a horrible mess—musically speaking, anyway." She paused, recalling something vaguely. "Wasn't this—"

"Yeah, it's the same thing Stan sent my dad by courier last weekend. He must've written it up and kept a copy before he left Washington."

"The only problem now is deciphering a code. I mean, is it in the notes? How do we read it? Left to right, bottom to top?"

"Or is it the chords themselves?" Doug mused, figuring if Stan had gone to all this trouble to hide a coded message, he wouldn't make the message easy to find. "Since Stan and Dad were both string players, it is odd he wouldn't identify the chords by name and number—because that's all guitar players have on their music."

"Well, then, I guess right there we've got two ways to go," she said. "Do you want to take the notes or the chords?" She jumped up and went to the desk in the corner, getting paper and pens for both of them. "I figure if we write it all out, we can give it to Billy—" She stopped at the chagrined look on his face. "What's wrong?"

"I, uh, I can't identify chords," Doug admitted, thoroughly embarrassed to have to tell her that when she already had such a low opinion of musicians. "Or read bass clef."

She stared at him, motionless. "You're kidding."

He felt himself flushing. "No. I'm a trumpet player. I—"

"They didn't teach you in college?"

And now for the second-worst revelation, Doug thought. "I didn't go to college."

"Oh."

That subdued her all right. He could see that she was thinking it was another difference between them. Not only was he a drifter, in her opinion, but an uneducated one.

"You didn't want to go to college?" she asked, moving more slowly toward him. They took the music and settled on either side of the piano bench.

Doug shook his head, telling her that wasn't the way it was. "I wanted to go, more badly than you can imagine, but my dad thought it was a waste of time. He felt music was an avocation not a vocation, and he refused to pay for my tuition unless I chose a serious major—one where I could get a 'decent' job. Something like engineering or programming."

"I knew he was trying to protect me, of course, do what he thought was best. I also knew he was wrong. Dead wrong, in this instance. So I left home."

"At eighteen?"

Doug nodded, the memories anything but happy now. He sobered, encouraged to go on only by the compassion and understanding he saw on her face. "I won't pretend those first years on my own were anything to write home about. They were lousy. I was always broke. I had to scramble for every job. For ten years I played in every hellhole from coast to coast, and although it wasn't comfortable in any sense of the word, I did learn. I learned a hell of a lot about style and technique and artistry."

"It shows when you play," she said softly, meaning it.

He glowed from her praise. "Anyway, when I was twenty-six I started getting jobs as a session musician for recording artists. I played background music and started making a decent living. Finally I was able to put my own band together, and now we play several months a year in the more exclusive clubs in Vegas, New York, L.A."

"Your father must be proud of you now."

Doug shrugged. "I don't know. I don't think—deep down—any of it has ever really impressed him. He loves me, but in his gut I think he still wishes I'd done something more traditional. Like Billy or Pam."

"Has he said that to you?"

"No, but I can look at his face and tell what he's thinking." Doug was quiet a long moment. His voice roughened emotionally and dropped another notch. "I was hoping that would change when he heard me play again. That's one of the reasons Pam arranged this get-together for us here. She knew I had a gig here and she figured it was a good time for Dad to view my success. And then, too, he had a rough year of his own."

"Like what?"

"He was passed over for promotion again. Pam thinks he'd finally begun to lose his rose-colored view of the military life and might accept the choices I'd made. I didn't really know if that was true, but I was willing to find out. As I said, I'm not that close to my dad. We talk, but never about anything that important, at least not lately. I love him, but—" Doug's voice broke, and he couldn't go on. Needing a moment to himself, he pushed away from the table.

Marianne gave him time to collect himself, then went to comfort him. She seemed to know instinctively how he must feel; isolated, afraid, worried. She put her arms around his waist and rested her cheek against his shoulder. She could feel his heart beating, slowly and steadily, against her face.

"I'm sure your dad is proud of you. Maybe he doesn't agree with your choice of careers. So what? No parent ever entirely approves of his children." She drew away slightly, so she could better see his face. "My mother and stepfather, for instance. They want me to be married."

"Is that why you're so intent on only romancing suitable mates?" he teased, taking the opportunity to change the subject entirely.

She pressed her lips together, deciding to sidestep that question altogether. "Back to the music," she said crisply. "We have clues to uncover."

Two hours later, they had identified every chord and every note. But they had nothing at all. If there was a pattern or a readily identifiable code, they couldn't see it. "I think it's time to call in Billy," Doug said, sighing. He admitted he was disappointed. He had wanted to decipher this all by himself.

Marianne reluctantly agreed. As much as she enjoyed sleuthing, she could see they weren't getting results. And time for his father could be running out.

She began gathering up the stacks of old music. They were all yellowed with age in varying degrees, and some were quite fragile. Preparing to put them in the bench, she thought she saw lightly penciled numbers in the top right hand corners. She looked again. "Doug? What are these?"

He glanced at the numbers. "Song orders, for their gigs." He looked again, and saw there were more pencil markings on the songs—an occasional note pointed out specifically, a numbered measure. "Do you think it means anything?" Marianne asked.

"I don't know," Doug said. "But there's one way to find out."

First, they arranged the stack of music in order, then they began writing out all the pencil marks, in the order in which they occurred. Within minutes, they had a pattern.

Marianne read it out loud: "CGBI, 2-1, DC1. CGB2, 2-7, DC3. BAE, 3-18, DC 4. CGB2, 3-29, DC1. CGB1, 4-3, DC5. CGB2, 4-6, DC1." And on it went.

"What do you think it is?" she asked.

"I don't know. But it looks like it's in chronological order—if those numbers are dates, and I think they might be."

"Do you think the other initials are names?"

"Maybe. Whatever, it does look like my dad and Stan were working on a case—despite Keel's claim to the contrary." Doug's mood and tone were suddenly grim.

"And they were going to plenty of trouble to keep the data they uncovered secret," Marianne said.

"Which supports a theory of a leak somewhere in the NIS," Doug theorized.

"So what do we do next?"

Reading her mind, Doug said, "Billy's already tied up with the notebook."

Marianne frowned, troubled. She guessed Doug was right. They probably did need to split up this data. "What should we do about the music?"

Doug was silent, thinking. He had taken care of the notebook easily enough, but there wasn't room in his trumpet case to hide this huge stack of music.

"What if we put it in a safety deposit box?" he suggested. "Do you have one?"

"Sure. You really think it's necessary?" Part of her thought it was, the other part of her felt that because of all that had happened she and Doug were now overreacting to everything.

"I know it may sound paranoid, but I can't shake the gut feeling my dad is in grave danger." Doug regarded her steadily, his voice dropping to a whisper. "Maybe we all are."

THE ROOM WAS SMOKY, and cluttered with half-filled coffee cups and stale pastry. The two men had been up most of the night, bent over the small tape recorder, listening to the information being unknowingly broadcast from two floors above.

"He can implicate us," the swarthy man said, taking a swig from the flask of vodka he kept in his pocket.

"Only if he is alive," said the second calmly.

"We cannot kill him if we cannot find him, comrade."

"Joseph will surface eventually—to see his family."

"Perhaps. Perhaps not. What are we going to do in the meantime?" the swarthy man lit a cigarette.

The blond agent grinned, his smile icy, remorseless. "We will find that safety deposit key. Once we have the music they have uncoded...."

The second agent smiled and fingered the ice pick he carried with him. It had been very easy, planting that listening device. Almost too easy. Even for the bumbling American "help" they had enlisted. They'd been able to hear everything that had gone on in Marianne Spencer's apartment the night before. "And the woman?" he asked, already knowing the answer, relishing the time when he would have her alone. Before her death. "What will we do with her in the meantime?"

"We must make sure she does not talk."

The swarthy man took another deep, contemplative drag of his cigarette. The thought of the red-haired woman at his mercy pleased him. They would not have much time together, but he would use it well. "And the musician?" Now that one, more than any of the others, he thought, was in the way.

His comrade shared the opinion as he decided, his eyes bleak and pitiless. "When we have the information, he, too, must die."

## Chapter Nine

"The next problem is how to get the music out of here without arousing suspicion," Doug said, once the music was in neat stacks. "I don't think you should just go straight to your safety deposit box. That's a little too obvious."

Marianne saw where he was leading. "On the other hand, if I were to get dressed and go into the office for a few hours, and then do some casual errands on my lunch hour—one of them being to run to the credit union—that probably wouldn't rate a second glance."

"Do you have your briefcase here?"

Marianne grimaced. They'd just found the first hole in their plan. "I left it at the office yesterday. But I think I may have my old one. Although where I would have put it..." Her voice trailed off. "It's probably still in the bedroom closet."

Doug groaned, envisioning the search ahead of them. "Is that one as bad as the hall closet?"

"Worse."

He followed her into the bedroom, and soon found himself holding books and magazines, even a spare suitcase or two.

Standing on a metal folding chair, she had almost reached the briefcase at the top when she lost her balance and tipped over a stack of things. Without warning, everything on the top shelf came tumbling down.

"Well, I got it." Marianne tossed him the battered old briefcase.

"Great," Doug said, rummaging through shoe boxes, scarves, a picnic hamper. He continued to eye the wicker basket contemplatively, keeping it aside. "Now you can put all the rest of this stuff back."

"Thanks heaps," she said dryly, curiously peering inside a shoe box that seemed peculiarly to have escaped the thick layer of dust that coated everything else in her closet. "I—" Her breath caught in her throat and then blew out in a choked whisper. "Oh, my God...what is this?" She stared down at stacks of crisp green bills.

Doug came toward her, his expression concerned. "What?"

"Money!" she whispered excitedly, resisting the urge to jump up and down. "Look at all this money! Is it real?"

Doug moved closer to get a better look. "It looks real enough. Feels real."

"Doug, how did this get here?"

He sobered instantly at her suddenly frightened tone. "I don't know. Last night maybe?"

"Of course. That's why the apartment was in such good shape. They didn't want to steal anything from me, but to plant something." She looked at him. "What about your hotel room? Pamela's and Seth's? Were they broken into?"

"I don't know. We've had someone in the family there, keeping an eye on things, but I suppose it's possible."

A mixture of panic and surprise was coursing through her veins. "What are we going to do?"

"I don't know. I have to think. The first thing, I guess, is get rid of the money."

She knew he was right. It did look incriminating.

"How?"

"I don't know. We'll think of something. And we have to check my room, too."

"All right." They were still whispering. Her heart was beating triple time. Beyond the nerves, though, was the awareness that she was very glad he was with her. It seemed like the enemy—whoever that was—had all the advantages. "When should we go?"

"Right now. But forget going into the office." Doug picked up the dusty wicker basket, and smiled slowly. "I think I have an even better idea."

WITH MARRIANNE DRESSED in shorts, the heavy picnic basket draped over her arm, and Doug tagging along beside her, fishing gear in hand, they left her apartment building. Both had on sunglasses and hats. For protection, Doug had insisted on putting a sharp knife, a police whistle and a can of Mace in the basket. Marianne had strapped on a beeper that she could use to alert security of her whereabouts. Nonetheless, despite the measures they'd taken to protect themselves, they were still uneasy. Sure they were being followed, they flirted and laughed as they walked the short distance to her car. As far as either could tell, they were alone. For the moment anyway.

And yet they remained tense.

Pretending to powder her nose, Marianne used her compact as a rearview mirror and glanced surreptitiously at the road behind them. She saw no vehicles following theirs, and traffic was light enough in the small residential area of the park to make it obvious if someone was. She began to relax ever so slightly. Maybe she was being imaginative. Yet there was the money that had been put in her apartment, and the two attacks she'd endured in as many days.

She was right to be afraid.

First stop was the CWR employees credit union, where Marianne's safety deposit box was located. She took the package containing the music inside, and quickly locked it in her box. She pocketed the key and returned to the car where Doug was waiting. She knew she had been fairly obvious, but she was in a hurry to get rid of the money, and she wanted the music safe in the meanwhile. They'd agreed the stop at the bank was a risk they had to take.

The next stop was Doug's hotel room. Briefly, they explained to Seth, Pam and Billy what was going on. The alarm on their faces was tangible. A quick search of all four rooms ensued; Three rooms were clean. Doug wasn't so lucky.

Taped to the underside of the box spring on his bed, Marianne found a small camera, no bigger than a pack of cigarettes. It was filled with unused, reel-type microfilm.

"What do you think this means?" Marianne said, her heart pounding in her chest. She felt like she was the target of some scam, and that at any minute everything would come crashing down upon her shoulders.

Pam, Seth and Billy wandered in through a connecting door seconds after the discovery was made. They whitened, seeing the discovery.

Doug stared at the camera, his jaw rigid. "Obviously someone wants to frame me, as well as my dad."

"Who's been in here?" Marianne asked.

Billy shrugged. "No one I know of."

Pam puzzled over the problem. "I can understand someone wanting to frame Doug. He's Joe's son, after all. And maybe the reason my father is on the run is that *he's* being framed. Possibly by someone at the NIS. But why you, Marianne? Why would someone be after you?"

Billy watched Marianne, making no immediate judgment as to her guilt or innocence. "Something very strange is going on here," he murmured slowly.

Marianne sighed. "Clearly someone wants to implicate me," she said slowly, "but for what? What have I done?"

Doug continued to look grim. "Let's all calm down, stop speculating and review what we know," he said tersely. "My dad works for the NIS, so did Stan. Dad is missing. The circumstances of Stan's death are suspicious, to say the least—"

"And now we're being framed," Marianne cut in impatiently. "You and I, Doug. But why us?" Why not Pam and Seth and Billy? she wondered. "We're not doing anything except—" the truth dawned on her slowly "—trying to find out what happened."

"And obviously making quite a nuisance of ourselves. We must be getting close to the truth or we wouldn't be perceived as such a threat."

"So what now?" Marianne whispered, beginning to feel really afraid. This was like a nightmare that just wouldn't end.

"I think we should get rid of the money and the camera," Doug whispered back. "All of it, and the sooner the better."

Marianne was silent, considering what he had proposed. It went against everything she had ever believed; she was a person who worked with the system, not around it. Her first instinct was to turn everything over to the Cypress City police and level with them. Surely they'd believe her, she thought. But what if she was just being naive? What then? If Marianne was somehow connected with Stan's death or Joe's disappearance, however falsely, she could end up going to jail. Suddenly, that wasn't a risk she was willing to take.

"SORRY TO BOTHER YOU, Ms. Granger, but we've got a major problem over here at the CWR credit union. I think we nearly had a robbery here today."

Nina stopped making notes on the pad in front of her and gave all her attention to the security guard on the phone. "Go on."

"Well, a couple of maintenance men came in, and arranged for a safety deposit box for each of them, and then went in to put some personal papers in the boxes. They seemed to be taking an awfully long time, so the clerk at the desk sent another guard to check on them. He found one of them trying to break into another deposit box."

As the full impact of what he said hit her, Nina Granger felt her blood pressure rise. How was that possible? "Where were the guards?" she demanded agitatedly.

As she became more upset, the guard became calmer. "Well, ma'am, evidently the one that accompanied the two men into the vault was knocked out by this other fellow—the, uh, bogus maintenance man. Hit right over the head."

"How do you know he was bogus?" Nina demanded impatiently.

"Because later the two guys' paperwork didn't check out. They were using employee serial numbers that belonged to other people."

"Did you arrest the imposters?" That was all they needed, men running around with false badges. She wondered briefly who they were. Company men, perhaps? Were these people linked to Joe? Or were they linked to her... and her past?

She forced herself to calm down.

"Nah, we didn't get them. They both got away. But you can rest easy. Nothing was stolen. They didn't even open the box they were trying to get into."

"Whose box were they were trying to break into?" Maybe this would be a clue, Nina thought.

"Marianne Spencer's. It was probably just a random theft, but you never know. You wouldn't happen to know where she is, would you? We called her apartment but there was no answer, just her machine."

"No. She has the day off." Nina's hand was shaking as she tapped a cigarette out of the pack and tried to light it. "Look, forget trying to contact her. There's no need to upset her until we know a little more, anyway. I'll come right over and check it out."

"Do you know what this is about?" the security man asked suspiciously.

"I'm afraid I do," she said briskly. "This is a highly confidential matter." She paused and swallowed hard.

"The United States Navy is involved. Therefore, it's of utmost importance we keep this quiet. Pass that along to the employees there, and make damn sure no one talks. How many already know about it?"

"Five, maybe ten."

Nina groaned inwardly. "Well, see that they're all told to keep quiet. If they don't their jobs could very well be on the line. And I'll tell Marianne," she lied, knowing this bending of the truth was absolutely necessary if she wanted to ensure her own safety.

"Whatever you think best."

"Close the area off entirely—no one in or out of the safety deposit vault for the rest of the day." That would buy her time, but how much?

She hung up, feeling the quaking of her limbs begin in earnest. Stubbing out the cigarette, Nina grabbed her purse.

She couldn't do this alone.

Her decision made, she stepped out of her office and walked down to use the pay phone in the lobby. It took only moments to get Commander Keel on the line. "Craig," she said hotly, "we've got trouble."


"THE LAST THING I thought I'd be doing today was going fishing," Marianne said, checking the security beeper attached to her belt.

"What better place to dump this than in the middle of Bay Lake?" Doug asked, motoring the rented speedboat to the center of the lake. Miles from other boaters, he had turned off the motor and put down anchor.

"Got me there," Marianne said, smiling.

Billy was in another speedboat, roughly half a mile away. On cue, he drove past five minutes later, splashing them with his wake. Marianne screamed as the water hit her face; Doug yelled, too, and leaning forward, carefully sent the plastic-wrapped, waterproofed package hurling surreptitiously over the side of the boat and down into the eighty-foot depths of the lake. Inside was the money and the camera.

Exhilarated to have accomplished the task, they motored back to the dock and turned the rented boat in. At the dock, Marianne received a message from her boss, who apparently with great difficulty had tracked her there.

"Bad news?" Doug asked.

Marianne shrugged. "Seems they're suddenly short-handed over at guest relations. My boss wants me to go back in until eight." She glanced at her watch. It was after four now. It was a ten-minute drive from the docks to her office. She had clothes there; she could change in the private bath off her office.

"And after that?" Doug asked, disappointment on his face.

Marianne smiled. Now that she'd had a taste of what a normal day with Doug could be like, more or less, she was reluctant to give up her time with him. Besides, he wouldn't be here forever. Maybe it wasn't such a bad deal to grab happiness when and where it appeared. Even if the bliss went with him, she would have her memories. "After that I'm free," she said softly.

"I don't have to work tonight, either. What do you say we have dinner together? I could pick you up at your office at eight. We can go somewhere in the park."

There was no way she could ignore the warmth and steadiness of his presence. "All right," Marianne said slowly, wondering even as she spoke if she was doing the right thing, getting even more involved with Doug than she already was.

On the other hand, considering the danger she was in, wouldn't it be crazy not to spend time with him? Who knew what bedlam the evening would bring? Staying with Doug was the safest possible route to take—for the moment, anyway. Together, they could fight their enemies. Alone, they were vulnerable. Until they'd unraveled the mystery and ended the cycle of violence and betrayal, they would have to remain partners. Because until then, like it or not, they were involved, their lives tangled and meshed—irrevocably.

## Chapter Ten

Nina waited until she and Commander Keel were alone in the vault before she spoke her thoughts. "Can you get into Marianne's safety deposit box?" Craig asked.

Nina shook her head slowly. "You know I can't. That's against the law." In fact, she was violating ethics just by telling Keel what had gone on at the credit union. But what else was she going to do? She was scared. It seemed like her past—or something very similar—was coming back to haunt her. To expose her. To hurt her. And she didn't want to start moving and running and hiding again. It had taken her too long to build up just this precious little security.

"The law isn't going to help us much now."

"I can't get into her deposit box. Not without notifying the bank president. And for propriety's sake, he'd probably want Marianne here."

"And ten to one she wouldn't want us to know about whatever she put in the box."

Nina sent him a worried look. Years ago she'd suffered from a stress ulcer. She felt the sour burning feeling begin again in her stomach. "*If* she's now working with Joe. We don't know that for sure. What if she's innocent?"

"Come on, Nina. Grow up. You've seen people chin deep in scams before. And you haven't hesitated to act."

She'd been young then. And innocent to what could happen to her or any others. But her naïveté had faded the moment she'd seen her best friend get blown up in her car. She'd known that bomb was meant for her. And she still had to live with the death on her conscience. Like she'd have to live with any more deaths now. "I don't want to be involved," Nina insisted stubbornly, wishing smoking were permitted in the vault.

"You are involved," he returned.

"Wrong. I just don't want to see the resort hurt."

Craig's pale amber gaze narrowed. "Your job jeopardized, you mean. Or your cover."

She caught a subtle hint of malice in his gaze. She watched him pick a speck of lint off his impeccably creased trousers. She had learned before what an ambitious man Craig Keel was. He'd let nothing, no one stand in his way.

"You're not doing anything to Marianne," he said smoothly, his voice dropping a convincing notch. "Or Joe's son. Not anything they haven't already done to themselves, anyway. From the looks of it, I'd say those Maitlands are all thick as thieves, and in this every bit as deep as their father."

Commander Keel cast a look over his shoulder. He tapped his foot impatiently. Outside the vault, he had two armed Navy men standing guard, as well as the security men Nina had already spoken to.

"All right," Nina said finally, knowing she couldn't stop him from doing what he wanted anyway. The only thing she could do was keep his actions quiet—and hence, keep her name and face out of it, at least publicly. Keel grinned and set about picking the lock. It was a difficult one, but he managed it in about seven minutes.

Sweat streaming down his brow, he took the box into a private viewing room. Nina followed nervously, sure they were about to be discovered. Part of her said she never should have alerted him to the theft, the other half of her knew Craig Keel was the only one who could save her from more terror. And she just couldn't go through that again, live the way she had that last year in Washington, D.C.

Beside her, Keel was already swiftly and methodically rifling the contents of the deposit box, which was filled to the brim. He pulled out a brand-new manila envelope, thick with papers.

With a victorious grin, Keel opened it. Inside were pages upon pages of dog-eared music that had been yellowed with age.

Nina nervously watched the door. If only he would hurry! "Does any of it make any sense to you?" she whispered harshly, her voice shaking, her face pale.

"It looks like some sort of code," he said finally.

"What are you going to do with it?" Nina whispered. She clenched her fists, willing him to make up his damn mind quickly!

But to her dismay, he was lost in his own thoughts. And it was fear.

"What do you think I'm going to do?" he snapped back irritably, unbuttoning his starched uniform shirt and sliding the envelope between his T-shirt and skin. "I'm taking it with me."

"You can't do that! Then she'll know someone broke in."

"I'm not stupid, Nina. I have no intention of keeping this indefinitely. Just long enough to copy the papers. Then you can put them back. After all, we'll need proof of the duplicity and conspiracy in order to convict. And now that I know where the evidence is and will be again, I can easily get a search warrant. I'll be a real hero, just like before."

She watched as he adjusted his clothing so the envelope didn't show. "You think it's that incriminating?"

"Trust me. It's incriminating as hell," Keel said roughly.

"How long will it be before you make an arrest?" Were they heading for another trial? If so, she was opting out, because she'd be damned if she'd go to jail. No, she'd rather live anonymously than go back to the hell of a trial with full newspaper coverage. She knew enough about living life one step ahead of the others now. Without friends. Without family. Without anyone.

"I don't know!" Crag shot back irascibly.

Aware they'd been in there way too long, Nina replaced everything else and put the box back in place.

That accomplished, she put on a bright, calm, professional mask. She and Craig left the vault, repeatedly reassuring everyone in the credit union who knew of the attempted theft that everything was all right. To her relief, everyone, including the Navy men bought it. Obviously, the Commander was trusted implicitly—at least by the men he'd drafted to protect him.

They parted company as soon as they left the credit union, Craig going with his military guards. Nina was escorted back to her office by two CWR security men, and again, for their benefit, she put on a calm appearance.

She didn't know where Craig intended to put the papers they had found; she only sensed they would be safe, where no one else would possibly be able to get them. For the moment her past was still a secret.

But Marianne...Marianne was treading on the edge.

NORMALLY, MARIANNE ENJOYED her work—so much so that it was sometimes hard to go home at the end of the day. But Saturday night was different. She could hardly concentrate. For one thing, Nina Granger was acting awfully weird. She'd been irritable with Marianne, almost suspicious, grilling her on where she had been with Doug and why. Then, out of the blue, she'd warned Marianne to be careful how involved she got with the Maitlands, and Marianne had sensed a caution that went far beyond her sensible words.

It was almost as if Nina sensed what was happening to her. But that was impossible.

She kept thinking about Doug, how he'd look as he was masterfully taking command of the boat, how it had felt to be kissed and held and, yes—rescued by him. Although she still had reservations about the wisdom of her decision, she was beginning to see some sort of liaison with him was inevitable. They couldn't stay away from one another, and even if they tried, events kept throwing them together.

"Ms. Spencer?" The low voice jerked her out of her reverie and she looked up to see a man standing in the doorway. "I'm Tom Merchant. I was told you might help me."

Marianne glanced at her watch; Doug was due to pick her up in five minutes. But as always it was work before pleasure. She stood, extending her hand in greeting. The man was in his early to mid thirties. Of medium height, slender build, he had dark blond hair, worn so it brushed his collar and completely covered his ears. "What can I do for you?" she asked pleasantly, noticing that with his beard and mustache, the lavender Van Halen shirt and white shorts, Tom Merchant looked more the quintessential musician or artist than Doug Maitland did.

"I'm here to report a theft. Mind if I sit down?" He gestured to the chairs in front of her desk.

"Please do," Marianne said, already reaching for a pencil and forms. "What was stolen, Mr. Merchant?"

"My camera." He paused, his distress showing, and swallowed hard. "It's a really good Nikon, a gift from my father."

"You're sure it's not misplaced?" she asked gently.

"No, and here's the weird part. I mean, I almost couldn't believe it happened, you know what I mean?" As he talked, a faint southern drawl crept into his voice. "I was in one of the camera shops on Main Street in the Enchanted Village, buying film for my camera. I bought about ten rolls. I'm an amateur photographer and I was hoping to get some photos to enter into some of the competitions in Biloxi—that's where I'm from. Okay, with me so far? Well, I walk out of the shop." He stood to demonstrate. "I've got my camera case on my arm and these two foreign dudes come up and rip the damn thing right off my arm!"

Alarms sounded in Marianne's head. The men who'd pulled her off the Space city ride and drugged her had accents. It had been too dark in the room to see their faces, but perhaps they were the same two. "Did you try to stop them?"

"Of course I tried to stop them, but that horse-drawn trolley came around just then. They cut across before it passed. By the time I got past it two seconds later they had disappeared into the crowd."

"Did you tell security?"

"Yes." His tone became defensive, and then a little angry. "They couldn't help. So they sent me here to you, said I could fill out a lost-and-found report, maybe collect some insurance on it."

"Well, I can give you the report to fill out. But as for the insurance, that's between you and your insurer. Children's World assumes no responsibility for the property of its guests."

"So I heard," he said dryly.

She handed him the forms and he began the laborious process of filling them out.

"Mr. Merchant, what did these two men look like?" Marianne asked.

"Uh, one was tall and blond, really skinny, real light, almost white-blond hair. The other was just a little bit shorter, maybe five eleven or so, with a build like a wrestler, if you know what I mean. And, man, he was strong. About tore my arm off when he yanked that camera."

"Did anyone else see what happened?"

"I don't know."

"You didn't yell at them to stop or anything like that?"

"Uh, no. I—" he looked sheepish. "I guess maybe I should have, but it all happened so fast."

"It might have helped; then again maybe not. It's hard to say." Marianne comforted him the best she could. "I am sorry."

"Yeah, well, so am I." Tom sighed and looked at the detailed form in front of him.

"If we're to help you we need a complete report."

Before Tom could respond, Doug appeared in the doorway, rapped lightly on the frame. "Hi." He cast a look at Marianne, then one at her guest. "Still working?" His glance came back to rest on Marianne.

She felt warmth sluice through her in waves. "Almost done."

"Good." His eyes held hers.

Before he could speak again, they were interrupted and Marianne went out to attend to a lost child. Doug went with her. The five-year-old was comforted by their calm, cheerful presence, and after a series of questions, Marianne was able to figure out her family was staying at the wilderness campgrounds.

Without warning, Tom Merchant appeared in the door of the lounge. "Ms. Spencer? I'm going to be taking off now. I left the report on your desk."

"That's fine, Mr. Merchant. And I'll let you know if I hear anything about your camera."

It was another hour before the little girl's parents, tearful and upset, showed up to claim their daughter. "Some night." Doug sighed when they were finally alone.

Marianne nodded. All she wanted was a hot bath and some quiet time alone with Doug.

"Still game for that dinner?"

"Sure. Why not?"

Half an hour later, they were ensconced in a cozy booth on the second floor of the Japanese restaurant, eating tempura. In the candlelight, Marianne could see the sunburn on his face. Had it only been that afternoon they'd dumped the money and the camera over the side of the boat? She felt it had been an eternity since she had been with him.

She missed him, she realized slowly. And that was a first.

"You really like your work, don't you?" he said softly.

She nodded, her eyes holding his. "It's very satisfying."

He slipped his hand over hers. "You were very good with that little girl." His tone was low, impressed.

Marianne smiled, feeling an inner glow at his praise. She wanted him to respect her, she realized, and the depth of her need for his approval surprised her. "So were you." She sipped her wine, and aware he was still watching her, looked over at him with a half smile. "Do you want children?" She wasn't sure why that was so important, only that she needed to know now.

He nodded slowly, his eyes turning a molten silver. "Yeah. I do." The hand on hers tightened. "What about you?"

"Two. A girl and a boy."

"Not ten?" he teased.

She shook her head negatively. "Not even a half dozen." There were limits, after all, to what working mothers could do.

He shifted his legs, inadvertently and briefly brushing hers. "How long have you worked at the park?"

A long time, she thought, wondering suddenly where all the years had gone. "Since I got out of college."

"Expect to be a vice president here someday?"

"Maybe." She smiled slowly. "What about you? What do you want?"

He stared at her intently. "I don't know," he said finally, taking her hands in his. "I do know that I'm tired of living out of a suitcase. But beyond that..." His words trailed off.

She looked away, aware her pulse was racing, and that funny feeling was right back in her middle.

A shadow loomed over them. A waiter bowed slightly and said, "Ms. Spencer? There's a call for you."

"Thank you." Marianne apologetically picked up the phone. She was always busy, but she didn't think she'd ever had this many phone calls in her life, or wanted the disturbances and distractions less.

"An executive's job is never done," Doug quipped as she hung up moments later. Then, seeing the funny look on her face, he asked, "What is it?"

Marianne shrugged, already gathering up her purse. "There's an envelope for you waiting at my office. It just came, special delivery. The doorman downstairs is holding it."

They didn't even have to discuss it; they both knew what they wanted to do. The minute they finished paying for their meal, they headed for Marianne's office. Marianne thought en route that perhaps it was just as well their romantic interlude had been interrupted. She was too close to falling head over heels in love with Doug. Oh, who was she kidding? She was in love with Doug. And their being too different to make it work wouldn't change the way she felt. She would just have to learn to deal with it, to not react on feelings, as her mother had, but on common sense as she knew she should. The only question in her mind was could she do it? Because every time she was with him, every second, her guard was reduced a little more.

As promised, the building doorman was holding the envelope. "Who brought this over?" Marianne asked, wondering if maybe Doug's father had made an appearance.

"Federal Express."

Doug scanned the envelope and bill carefully. "It was sent from Cypress City."

"A lot of trouble and expense, considering Cypress City's only twenty miles away," Marianne mused.

Doug looked at her anxiously. She could tell his mind was spinning, too. "Mind if we go up to your office to read this?"

She agreed, and they headed for the elevators. The minute the doors were shut, she asked, "What's the return address?"

Doug whitened even more. "It says Joe Maitland, and lists my dad's D.C. address." Suddenly, he didn't look all that anxious to open the envelope; he looked afraid.

The doors opened.

Swiftly, they started down the hall. They hadn't taken more than four steps when Marianne saw the mop bucket and cleaning cart outside her office. "So much for privacy," she said lightly. "Oh, well, we can use the lounge."

She caught a glimpse of the cleaning person as they zoomed past her office. He was dusting the chairs in front of her desk and didn't look up as she passed.

Marianne didn't interrupt him.

As he walked beside her, Doug kept his attention solely on the envelope. He had it open by the time they entered the lounge. "What the...?" he muttered, staring at the paper in his hands and sinking down onto the soft red leather sofa.

Marianne shut the door behind them and sat down beside him. "Ain't Misbehavin'?" she said, reading the title of the song he held in his hand.

Doug searched the envelope; there was nothing else inside.

Marianne took another look at the music. A mere two pages in length, it was marked up with all sorts of musical terms. Measure after measure of them. *Strettissimo, tremando, accelerando, yodel, obbligato, una tumultuoso...*

"Does that say yodel?" Marianne asked.

"Yodel," Doug affirmed, equally perplexed. They traded glances; obviously the musical terms were completely extraneous.

"Another code?" Marianne asked, her excitement growing.

"Maybe." Doug was pensive, not about to jump in until he'd considered all the angles.

"Let's go to my office," Marianne said briskly, already moving toward the door. If the cleaning person wasn't finished, then she'd tell him he'd done enough.

When they emerged from the lounge, however, the cleaning cart was nowhere in sight. Her office was empty. Marianne walked in, smelling the familiar scent of lemon wax and air freshener. She started for her desk, then stopped cold.

"What's wrong?" Doug asked, instantly picking up on her unease.

"The stolen merchandise report someone just filled out—that was over here, not—not in my out basket." She paused again, whirling around. On the surface, except for that one report, everything was in order. Her desk was locked up, as was her supply cabinet. The computer terminal beside her desk was cool. All her files were locked shut, with the exception of... Oh, no. Her heart began to pound as she yanked open the L-O drawer. She rifled through the manila folders rapidly, once and then again. Finished, she gave a low, distressed moan.

"Marianne, what is it?" he demanded.

"The file on your father." She swallowed hard and looked up at him, her eyes bright with fear. "It's missing."

# Chapter Eleven

The next hour was tense and unsettling for both of them. Once again, they had the feeling everything was out of their control and that by the time they caught on to what was going on, it would be all over, with Marianne and Doug possible casualties of the fray.

The only positive note was that the message from Doug's father turned out to be remarkably easy to decode. In fact, they figured it out in about ten minutes, as soon as they had written down all the extraneous terms in order, in a single column. Using the first letter of every musical term, in order, they deciphered a message that read, "Stay out of it, Blues. All of you. Classified."

Doug had no doubt his father had sent it. "Who's Blues?" Marianne asked, glad Doug was looking so happy, at least for a moment. She knew they weren't nearly out of trouble yet, nor was his dad, but at least they had done something right.

"He used to call me that when I was a kid," Doug murmured fondly. He got quickly to his feet and roamed her office excitedly, a spring in his step, his shoulders back. "Well, at least we know he's alive and that he knows what he's doing," Doug said, patting the doctored music against his palm.

Did he? Marianne only hoped so. "Why doesn't he contact you personally?"

"Maybe he can't."

"Are you going to stay out if it?" If Doug kept pacing like that, he would wear a hole in the carpet.

Doug turned toward her, his mood becoming sober. "That I don't know."

Marianne went back to study the message they'd written out on scrap paper. It hadn't been hard to pick out the terms. They'd stood out like neon letters. The trouble was it had been too easy. So much so that she couldn't shake the feeling they were still missing something. "Why do you think he went to all the trouble to cut these terms from a musical dictionary—at least I guess that's where he got them—and paste them on—rather than write them out himself?"

"I don't know." Doug shrugged. "Maybe he thought it would be easier and faster. Or maybe he thought he had to do something real obvious so I'd be able to decode the message."

Her head lifted curiously at the pique she heard in his tone. "You talk as if your father doesn't have much faith in you."

Doug's expression was troubled as he took a seat behind her desk, propping his feet up on the corner of the desk. Folding his hands in his lap, he admitted softly, "He doesn't have much faith in me. Or at least he didn't used to." His eyes turned cloudy with hurt. "I think the biggest disappointment of his life was my not choosing a career in the military."

Remembering the photo of Billy and his father the day Billy graduated from the academy, Marianne couldn't disagree. She could understand Doug feeling left out. "He must respect you now—"

Doug shrugged again and didn't answer. He turned the swivel chair around and briefly stared out the window. It was after midnight, and the park had closed. The horizon was a sea of darkness and twinkling lights, with the Magic Castle still visible. Sighing, he pushed his chair around so he faced her. "Any word on who that cleaning person was? You were on the phone quite a while."

"No one fitting that description works for the cleaning service in the executive building. The doorman didn't see anyone fitting that description, either."

"Meaning?"

"Meaning he probably stole a cart and broke into my office. And there's something else," she said, reluctant to give him more bad news. "That man who was in here earlier—he fits the description of one of the men who stole Tom Merchant's camera off his arm. I didn't think about it at the time. I was too intent on what was in the envelope your father had sent you. But later, I realized—"

"Is there anything else missing?"

"Just the file. Either he didn't try to break into my desk or he didn't have time."

"So what did he want? What's his connection to my father, and to Stan?" His gaze darkened. "Stan. In his file...?"

That Marianne hadn't thought to check.

It, too, was missing. Which meant whoever had it also had the autopsy report. She looked at Doug, wondering what they should do next.

He seemed to have a clear game plan in mind. "I think it's time we went to see my family."

PAM AND SETH WERE OUT when they arrived at the hotel. Billy was in his room, watching a ball game on television and eating a room-service dinner.

He was elated at receiving the message they'd deciphered. "At least we know Dad's all right."

Doug sent a disapproving look at the portable computer not currently in use. "We'd know a hell of a lot more if you'd just break that code in Stan's notebook, Billy."

Billy, as it turned out, wasn't in the best mood himself. "Hey, bud, I've been working night and day on this damn mess! Which is more than I can say for you!"

Marianne could see it was true; Billy had deep circles under his eyes. Like everyone else in the family, he looked exhausted and emotionally wrung out. "Apparently not hard enough," Doug growled.

"Just what are you accusing me of, Doug?" Billy stood abruptly, his fists balled at his sides, his jaw jutting out pugnaciously.

"Not trying," Doug said with a quiet virulence that made Marianne shiver. Before he could stop himself, the words he'd been suppressing all week came rushing out, "You want to know what I think? I think you don't really want to know what's in Stan's notebook."

Billy's eyes glimmered furiously. "Yeah?" he shot back sardonically, losing his temper, too. "Well, maybe you're right. Maybe I don't want to know. Maybe I don't think we have any business trying to decode it." He caught the strained, horrified look on Marianne's face and lowered his voice. "Look. I know you're anxious to find Dad, to make sure he's all right. So am I. But I don't want to do the wrong thing, either. I have a feeling decoding that notebook could be a fatal misstep."

Without warning, Pam and Seth entered the room.

Before Doug could change the subject, Billy said, "I told them about the notebook."

Pam was angry. "You shouldn't have kept it from me, Doug."

"You've been under a lot of strain." He'd only wanted to protect her, as he had when they were children.

"I don't need your protection. I need you to be honest with me. I thought we were a family." Taking a deep breath, she sent Doug a beseeching gaze. "The code is impossible, Doug. You haven't been here that much, but Seth and I have. Billy's been working his heart out trying to decode it, and he's getting absolutely nowhere."

"So?" Doug answered belligerently.

"So maybe that tells us Dad and Stan didn't want it decoded. Maybe whatever is in it is so sensitive it has to be kept under very tight security. Maybe we'd all be putting ourselves in even more danger if we know what it contains," Seth finished slowly, equitably holding Doug's gaze.

Doug surveyed his siblings and Seth. "What are you telling me? That you want to give up on Dad, too?"

"No," Billy said simply. "Just that we want Dad to come in on his terms, in his own time. We think we have to trust him, Doug. And so do you."

"I THOUGHT YOU WERE GOING to keep me informed on this," Nina shouted the moment Marianne walked in her office Sunday morning.

Marianne stood uneasily next to the door. It hadn't been a great night. Doug had stayed at his hotel, to go over the code. Knowing she'd had to go to work the next day, she'd finally gone home—alone—to sleep.

She had missed him. She hadn't slept well. And she sensed she wouldn't sleep well again for some time.

Those thoughts would hold; now, though, there were Nina's complaints to be dealt with. In all the time she'd known Nina, she'd never so much as raised her voice.

"No excuses, Marianne." Nina cut her off sharply, throwing down a stack of papers on her desk. "You either follow my instructions or you don't, and in this particular instance you didn't."

"I'm sorry I didn't tell you about the break-in at my office. It was an oversight. I had a lot to do," Marianne said finally. Among other things, she'd had to file the report on the missing camera, and as an extra precaution—in case he turned out to be in danger because he could identify the men who had robbed him—she had put a tail on him. Or at least she'd requested one. By the time she'd thought to do so, he'd already left his room for the day, but when he returned, he would be watched and guarded—surreptitiously, of course.

She'd offered the same service for the Maitlands, of course, but for the most part they had refused it, feeling Joe wouldn't try to contact them if he thought they weren't alone. So she'd had to content herself with posting security guards on the floor of their hotel, and down below. Anything else, at the moment, she just couldn't do.

In a calmer tone, Nina continued. "What's this I hear about a guest having his camera stolen in the Enchanted Village?"

Relieved to be able to discuss something other than her own ineptitude, Marianne launched into an explanation of Tom Merchant's visit to her office. "Naturally, he was shocked and upset," she finished.

"Were you able to get descriptions of the thieves?"

Marianne nodded. "I've circulated their descriptions to security."

"Did you call the Cypress City police?"

"No, not yet."

Nina relaxed slightly as she stubbed out her cigarette. "Good. I don't want the publicity either." She gave Marianne another hard look. "Think you'll be able to find that man's camera?"

"No." Marianne wouldn't lie to her boss, even to save her own neck. "But I'll give it my best shot."

Nina scrutinized her. "Be careful, Marianne," she said finally. "I don't know what's going on here. I'm not sure I want to know, or that you should know, either. But until things calm down, it'd pay to be extra careful. And keep me informed!"

On that note, she was dismissed.

But even after she left, Marianne couldn't get Nina's warning out of her mind. It was as if she knew something. Or feared something. But what? And why had she looked so frightened?

BECAUSE OF THE FAMILY'S escalating worries, Sunday evening was not the festive occasion the family had planned. It was Joe's fifty-fifth birthday, and they hadn't heard one word from him, except for the coded message he had sent. Nonetheless, the family gathered at the Mexican restaurant in the International Bazaar as they had originally planned.

Doug and Billy were crazy with anxiety, as were Pam and Seth, who had insisted Bryant tag along, too. Commander Keel, who was never very far behind any of them, was sitting in the cantina next to the reception area. Marianne, fearing the worst and hoping for the best, had tagged along, too.

"Should we have a second round of drinks?" Pam asked.

"Only if they're nonalcoholic," Seth said, still nursing his injured hand.

"Agreed," Doug said firmly, signaling the waiter. "We have to make this look as normal as possible." Even if they did have to drag a family dinner out for five hours, Marianne thought. At least CWR was picking up the tab for this, though. Nina had insisted upon it, and after all they'd been through, Marianne agreed.

Bryant turned and cast a disparaging look at Keel.

Doug picked up on it. "You don't like him much, do you?"

Bryant shrugged noncommittally. "We just seem to be at cross-purposes most of the time."

"What do you mean?" Marianne asked.

Bryant dipped a tortilla chip in salsa. "I want to find Joe and free him. Keel wants to convict him. I have a hunch Joe knows that, and it's why he's laying so low."

Marianne nodded slowly, still looking around. Although the waiter had brought plates of *queso fundida* as appetizers, she wasn't hungry. Neither was anyone else. They were largely an unenthusiastic, gloomy group.

She decided a change in subject was in order. "Did I detect a hint of southern drawl in your voice?" she asked Bryant. After he had had one drink, a margarita, which was rather hastily downed, she had noted he was drawing out his vowels.

Bryant grinned sheepishly and nodded, his alert eyes on hers for a flirtatiously long moment. "If you only

knew how hard I had worked to lose that rebel sound."
He sighed.

Marianne grinned. Having lived so many places herself as a child, she had developed no particular re-
gional accent. Nonetheless, she enjoyed a good
southern drawl. "I think it's charming."

Next to her, Doug raised a brow. Was he jealous?
Well, maybe she was laying it on too thick.

But Pamela seized on the diversion with the tenacity
of a drowning woman reaching for a life preserver. She
finished the last of her Virgin Mary. "Where are you
from again, Bryant? Georgia, isn't it?"

"Atlanta," he replied unenthusiastically, not looking up.

"Do you have family there?" Marianne asked. Anything to keep the conversational ball rolling and their
collective worries off Joe.

"Uh, yeah. A brother," Bryant answered, glancing
over at Keel, who was still sitting at the bar nursing a
diet Seven-Up.

"Is he with the FBI, too?" Doug asked casually, bit-
ing into a tortilla chip covered with salsa.

"No. He owns several nightclubs."

"Really," Doug said, leaning forward, intrigued.
"I've played in Atlanta. What are they called?"

Bryant seemed distracted; he couldn't take his eyes
off Keel, who was talking to the CWR guard. "Reflec-
tions I, II and III."

"Nice places," Doug commented. "How's he like
running clubs?"

"Fine."

Without warning, there was a commotion near the
front door. Marianne looked over to see a couple of
men in suits murmuring to the maître d'. It wasn't hard

to discern what was going on, even from a distance. The two men were trying to get in, obviously without reservations.

"Problem?" Doug asked.

Marianne nodded. "Looks like it." She was about to get up when she got a better look at the second man. She sucked in her breath.

"What is it?" Without warning, Doug was on his feet, too.

"That man. The heavy-set one with the dark hair. Isn't he the one who was cleaning my office?"

Bryant was on his feet automatically. Without a word of explanation to the others, he started toward the two foreign-looking men, fire in his eyes. Spying him coming their way, they took off, taking separate routes out of the place.

Bryant took off after the one who headed out the front door.

Doug moved swiftly between the tables, calling over his shoulder. "This way head out to the kitchen?"

"Yes," Marianne shouted back, keeping pace.

And then they were running, stumbling around waiters with trays. There was shouting as they passed through the kitchen. They dashed outside, into the fading sunlight and stifling heat.

The dark-haired man took off, running as fast as his girth would allow. Doug's pace picked up into a flat run. Marianne sprinted after him, catching up with the two of them precisely at the moment they fell to the ground. She screamed as they wrestled, flipping over and over. And then everything was happening at once. Tourists were surging forward, pulling the two men apart.

Marianne saw a photo slip from the swarthy man's pocket. She bent over to pick it up, surreptitiously sliding it up her sleeve. And then, before she could break it up, the foreigner landed an unexpected punch in the stomach of the man who had just rescued him from Doug, and was taking off again. Doug tried to follow, but was held back by the presence of several young children who'd wandered over to see what was going on. By the time he got past them the dark-haired man had disappeared.

Commander Keel pushed forward to Marianne's side. Looking at Doug, he swore. "You lost them. You're more like your old man than you know."

"That does it," Doug said, and then his fist went flying into Keel's jaw.

"YOU SHOULDN'T HAVE HIT the commander," Marianne said long moments later when they were back in the Mexican restaurant. She'd had the waiter bring Doug a damp hand towel, filled with ice, to put against the bruised knuckles of his right hand.

"She's right," Billy agreed. "What if he decides to press charges?"

"An assault charge is the last thing I'm worried about," Doug said.

"Yeah, well, at least we got rid of Keel," Seth said, taking a long swig of Mexican beer. "He makes me nervous."

"Me, too," said Pam, watching as Marianne, after shooting a cautious look around, carefully slid the photo out of her sleeve.

It was a black and white glossy of a blond-haired man—an American in his mid-thirties—giving a poster container to the swarthy man Doug had just tried to apprehend. He was clean-shaven, but she couldn't see much of his face because he wore sunglasses and a CWR cap.

"What is that?"

"It fell out of that guy's pocket," Marianne murmured. "I picked it up." She hadn't dared look at it earlier, because she hadn't wanted Keel to see that she had it. Only when she was once again in the protective circle of family did she dare look at it.

"Who's the guy in the CWR cap?" Doug asked.

"I don't know," Marianne murmured. He looked vaguely familiar, but she couldn't place him. She stared at the photo, wondering what it could mean. Was it blackmail of some sort?

Bryant walked back into the restaurant. Pamela gasped when she saw his face. He had a black eye and a jaw that was swelling up fast. Marianne signaled the waiter for more ice.

"Did you lose him?" Doug asked.

Bryant nodded grimly. "But not without giving it a good fight. It was the damn tourists. They intervened." He scowled at Marianne, muttering, "Where are the security guards when you need them?"

Choosing not to answer, she handed him the photo she had found. "What do you make of this?"

For a moment, Bryant didn't react. "Where'd you get this?" he said quietly, studying it with the mesmerized enthusiasm of a collector who's just been shown a stamp that might prove priceless.

Briefly, Marianne explained.

Bryant nodded, then looked at all the others. "Those two men who were just in here, they're suspected spies. They're wanted by Interpol and scores of other police for questioning. Needless to say, they're very dangerous. If you spot them again, don't give chase. Doing something like that could get you killed. In fact, if the park weren't so crowded today—''

Maybe one of them would already have died.

Marianne shuddered. "What should we do if we see them?" she asked.

"Call the police."

Bryant continued to study the photo. "Do either of these men look familiar?"

Marianne thought the dark-haired man resembled the cleaning man in her office the other night.

"What about the other one that was in here?" Bryant pressed. "The one not in the photograph. The tall skinny blond one. Have you seen him anywhere? Think, Marianne, it's important. Is it possible he's the one who broke into your apartment the other night, and tied you up?"

"I don't know." Marianne shuddered. "Maybe. But it was dark, and I was alone and I didn't really see..." It had all happened so fast.

Without warning, Pamela's skin assumed a greenish hue. Without speaking, she got up and ran off in the direction of the ladies' room.

Alarmed, Marianne followed. "You okay?" she asked when a shaken Pamela emerged from the stall. "If you want, I could call someone from first aid."

"No. Really, I'm fine now." Pam bent over the sink and rinsed her mouth. "Besides, Dad might show up. I want to be here if he does." Still looking a little shaky, Pam began rummaging through her purse. "I've got some makeup in here somewhere. Maybe that will help." Frustrated at not being able to find what she wanted immediately, Pamela pulled a whole handful of stuff out of her bag.

"That looks like the interior of my purse." Marianne grinned.

As she spoke, several papers fluttered to the floor. "You get the feeling this isn't my day?" Pam asked tiredly.

"I'll get them." Marianne knelt to pick up the mess. "You just put some color back into your face."

"Thanks." Pam turned back to the mirror.

Marianne never meant to look closely at any of the papers that had landed on the floor. But she couldn't help but notice the logo of a rival hotel corporation, and a sleazy one at that, on a transparent receipt. The date from the room was Saturday—two days before Pam supposedly arrived in Florida. Pam's name was the only one on the slip.

Pam, unnerved by the silence, slanted Marianne a glance.

"What's going on, Pam?"

Pam looked down at the receipt and got very quiet. "I needed time alone," she said finally. "Seth and I have had . . . personal difficulties."

Pam was hiding something. But what? "Did you and Seth have a fight? His hand—" The words slipped out before she could think. She paused, not sure how to phrase this without offending. "Pam, you didn't have anything to do with that, did you?"

Pam looked at Marianne. Her gaze was honest and compelling. "As a matter of fact, I do feel kind of responsible for that. You see, we'd been fighting so much and—" Her voice caught and trembled.

"About what?" Marianne asked quietly.

She swallowed hard, seeming to censor everything she said. "Money, mostly. I wanted to get married a very long time ago. Before Seth was even out of law school.

But he wanted to wait. He said being heavily in debt was no way to start a marriage. Anyway, he's been working a lot of overtime lately. He wants—needs—another raise. I got angry about never seeing him. We had this enormous fight. He stormed off, and it was after that he caught his hand in the door.''

''Did he blame you for what happened?''

She shrugged again. ''We both said a lot of things we didn't mean.'' She swallowed hard, as if finding it difficult to go on. ''I knew Dad and Doug were expecting us down here in a couple of days. I felt like I had to get away sooner, just to think. So I came down here. I took a cheap room near the airport, and just rested and—and thought about what to do next, how to—how to fix things. I didn't want anyone to know where I was or that there was trouble between me and Seth, so I didn't mention coming down here.''

''But you talked to Doug the night before you supposedly arrived.''

She nodded, gaining control of her emotions. ''Seth called me and told me Doug'd been trying to reach me. So I called and—well, I just told Doug I'd be there as soon as I could. It took me several hours to get myself together. I was a mess. I knew what time Billy's flight was coming in and I met him at the airport.''

''I see.''

''Do you? I love my family, Marianne, but some things are just too private. And Doug and Billy, not to mention Dad, sometimes they can be just too protective. Had Dad not disappeared the way he did, I probably would have talked to Doug, but as it was, by the time we got together, I felt he had enough on his mind. I just didn't want to make it worse. Please don't say anything to him about this. I'll tell him the truth, but later, after Dad has been found. Please, Marianne.''

"All right." Confronted with such a heartfelt plea, Marianne couldn't say anything else. Besides, she knew how it felt to have romantic troubles. And the last thing anyone needed was familial interference.

Pamela wasn't telling her everything, but that didn't necessarily mean anything. She didn't seem to know anything about what had happened to her father. She clearly cared about Joe. She loved her brothers. And despite the problems she was having with Seth, she obviously loved him.

For Marianne to think there was more to what had happened than what Pam had just explained was foolish. She was just overreacting, being overly suspicious because of all that had happened since the Maitlands arrived in Florida. Once Joe was found, Pam would quit keeping secrets and tell her brothers the truth, and everything would be fine.

## Chapter Twelve

"You're sure you don't want to go back to the hotel?" Doug asked.

"No, I'm fine.

"You're not ill?"

Pam took a deep breath and with difficulty held her older brother's gaze. "Not anymore. Will you relax?"

"How can I when we both know this isn't like you. And if it isn't the flu—" He stared at her for several considering seconds. "Okay," he demanded abruptly. "What's going on?"

"Nothing," Pam denied agitatedly.

"Has something happened we don't know about?"

Unexpectedly, he hit a nerve. A guilty flush spread from her neck into her face.

Casting a meaningful look at Pam, Seth intervened. "Hon, you don't have to tell him anything!"

"Maybe I want to," Pam countered, after taking a deep breath. She continued to hold Seth's steely gaze. "It's all going to come out sooner or later. They'll know and—" Ignoring her fiancé's beseeching gaze, she turned, looking at both brothers, then focusing on Doug. "I'm pregnant. I just found out last week. I—" She looked at Marianne, supplying the last pieces of the puzzle. "It wasn't something we planned on, and—well, I've been acting a little bit crazy." Tears welled up in her eyes. "Add to that the pressures from work, and this thing with Dad." The tears rolled down her face. She brushed them away with the back of her hand. "I just haven't known how to cope. I'm sorry if I worried you, but my sickness is nothing to worry about."

Seth nodded. "It happened twice in the past two weeks. That's what sent her to the doctor in the first place."

There was a silence around the table.

Suddenly Marianne understood so much, what Pamela had been hiding, what she felt she couldn't say, her fights with Seth about money and pressures, plus the fact they weren't married and were still heavily in debt. What had happened was bound to be upsetting.

Doug was the first to speak. "It's true? You're really going to have a baby?"

Pam smiled, looking both proud and shy. "Yes. I am. I know the timing is off. I don't know what Dad's going to think. Even if we got married today—well, everyone would know." She found that prospect embarrassing.

"Oh, who gives a damn," Billy jumped in with his usual profanity. "Congratulations, Sis and Seth!" He hugged her and his future brother-in-law. "A baby! How about that! Dad's going to be so pleased."

Bryant returned to the table. He'd been in the office, phoning in a report to his superiors and getting an APB put out on the two men. He said to Marianne, "That photo you picked up, I'd like to have it."

"I'll give you a photocopy," Marianne said.

Bryant looked stunned. "Why would you keep it?"

She looked at Doug. She wasn't sure those two men had anything to do with Joe's disappearance and Stan's death, but so far that explanation made more sense than anything else she could come up with. And if they had been working on a case undercover, as she and Doug had privately surmised… "Joe might need it, or be able to make some sense of it, if and when he does contact us, so I'd like to have it handy, just in case. Besides, I can put it in a safe place." She could fit it in her safety deposit box along with the music first thing the following morning.

Bryant was skeptical. "Where would it be safe? You've already had your apartment broken into, your office files burglarized. Come on, Marianne, you're not thinking logically."

"She sounds perfectly rational to me," Doug put in laconically, backing her up. "I vote we keep the original, Marianne."

Billy shrugged, not willing to hand over the photo, either. "I vote we keep it, too. I think Dad would want us to."

"I don't know, Marianne," Pam said finally. "What if just having that photo puts you in even more danger?"

"Who's going to know I have it but all of us?" Marianne said.

"True." Seth reached over and squeezed Pam's hand. "She's right. It'll be okay. And I'm sure Joe would want us to have it."

"You still haven't told us where you're going to put it," Bryant said.

Nor did Marianne intend to. She shook her head, not about to make her plans public knowledge to everyone within earshot. Maybe she was being paranoid, but she was beginning to feel she couldn't be too careful. "I'll get that copy for you," she said evasively, and walked through the restaurant to the manager's office and the copy machine within.

Bryant, seeing how determined she was to hang on to the photo, didn't try to dissuade her again. He left soon after, photocopy in hand.

Billy, impatient and worried, went out to prowl the front of the restaurant and the surrounding turf for any signs of his father or the thugs who had been there earlier. Pam and Seth, looking visibly more relaxed now that their news was out, stole a few quiet moments alone and walked over to browse through the open market adjacent to the restaurant.

Doug looked at Marianne. "I'm sorry this evening has been such a bust."

That he could be so tender, so concerned about her, when his own life was in such a shambles, touched her unbearably. "I'm sorry your father hasn't shown up yet," she said softly.

"It's nearing midnight," Doug noted with a sigh. He flexed his shoulders, trying to rid them of tension. "It doesn't look like he will." He touched her hand with his. "Thanks for holding on to that photo for me." His hand tightened over hers.

She reveled in the warmth. She might not want to acknowledge it, but there was a bond between them. And it grew stronger with every moment they spent together. She knew she would miss him terribly when he left, and that she'd always remember what time they did have.

"I was serious about what I said. Your father might need it."

"I know." Doug paused, his eyes clouding over. "It scares me to think of him in trouble."

"We have to believe he's all right, Doug."

"Yes, we do," he answered her stoically. But for Doug it was easier said than done.

DOUG AND MARIANNE WERE THE LAST to leave the restaurant, except for the maître d' and head chef. After long and careful deliberation, Marianne finally left the photo in an envelope in the restaurant safe, figuring she would transfer it to her safety deposit box sometime the next morning. A little paranoid, she and Doug looked over their shoulders the whole way back to her apartment. But no one followed them, no one lurked in the shadows. By the time she reached her building she'd begun to think they were both getting a little crazy and overimaginative under the strain.

Although it was after one by the time they reached her place, Doug seemed in no hurry to go home. She wanted him to stay, but she was afraid of what might happen if he did. And that being the case, she didn't feel she could invite him in for even a cup of coffee, for fear he would misconstrue her intentions and make a pass again.

"So this is it, hm?" he said at her door, reading the indecision and mixed emotions he saw on her face, the desire, the apprehension, that were as much a part of her nature as her common sense.

"I'm afraid so." She turned and slid the key in the lock.

His hand touched hers as her door swung open. The lazy predatory look was gone. In its place was a fiercely protective aura. "Hang on a minute, Marianne. Let me have a look around first. I want to make sure everything's okay."

She didn't refuse his offer. Since the break-in, she'd been jittery whenever she was in her apartment alone.

She told herself it was stupid. She hadn't been hurt before, and they'd gotten rid of the money. Still, she was nervous, but having Doug there helped.

She was laughing by the time he finished.

"You think it's funny, huh?"

She couldn't hold back a giggle. "There's a certain humor in having you crawling around the floor looking under my bed."

"Yeah, well—" He straightened laconically and handed her a single rumpled white sock. "I need to do it for me."

"I know." She laughed again, softly. And then suddenly his arms were coming around her, his mouth was coming down on hers. The kiss was fiery and explosive, a culmination of everything they had seen and experienced that night. She resisted him at first, in a mixture of surprise and confusion, but eventually, inevitably the passion took hold and soon she was returning his kiss. Marianne was shaking when he drew away.

"I should go now," he said. "But I really don't want to."

"But you will." Her voice was breathless but firm.

"Marianne—"

She knew what he was going to say: that he loved her. She saw it in his eyes, now and at the oddest moments: when they had been sitting in the Mexican restaurant and he'd thought she wasn't looking, when they had deciphered the code in "Ain't Misbehavin'." Whenever he walked toward her or was in her presence, the passion, the affection, were there.

But she couldn't, wouldn't let an involvement happen, she insisted stubbornly, knowing that the stakes got higher every minute. They were too different. They wanted different things out of life.

"You have to leave," she repeated sternly, extricating herself from his arms.

His expression was wary, unrepentant. "Sure you don't want a bodyguard here for the night?"

She knew all too well the offer included only what she wanted and nothing more. He wasn't the kind of man who would push, but he wouldn't let an opportunity pass to kiss her again, either. And the way she was feeling, she wasn't sure how much longer she could resist him.

Deciding a defensive tact was the safest, she took his hand and led him toward the front door. "Good night, Doug."

"Good night," he whispered softly, then backed her up against the door and delivered another long, soul-shattering kiss. His hands flat on the door on either side of her, his body touching hers length to length, he said softly, "You will transfer that photo tomorrow?"

"I promise, first thing tomorrow morning I'll get it put in an even safer place."

FOR THE SECOND TIME THAT WEEK, Nina was not alone in her apartment. But this time she'd already been in bed for the night when she thought she heard an uninvited intruder. Getting out of bed, she reached for the loaded gun she kept in her nightstand and started stealthily toward the kitchen.

She got no farther than the hall when the gun was knocked from her hand and a hand was clamped over her mouth. It all happened so fast, she didn't even have time to think, never mind struggle.

His arm in a choking vice around her neck, he reached down to recover the gun. "Hello, Nina," Joe Maitland said. "Long time, no see."

She straightened as he did, feeling the cold metal of the gun at her throat, the wall at her back. She knew it would do no good to scream. He could kill her before the sound even carried. She pressed her knees together to stop their shaking, and craved a cigarette. "What do you want?"

Taking a handful of her hair, he placed the gun at her back and propelled her toward a chair in the living room. "Let's you and I have a chat." His voice was anything but kind.

Anger began to take the place of fear. "Let's not."

His voice and grip got even more brutal. "Nina, sit, before I'm forced to do something unpleasant we'll both regret." He looked her up and down, pleased by the fearful acquiescence on her face. "Good. What does Keel know? And don't bother to deny anything. I know my sons are investigating—especially Doug. After all, it was his curiosity that got Keel down here in the first place."

The hair rose on the back of her neck. "How do you know that?"

"Because I still have some friends. Even if others would turn their backs on me." Becoming aggravated, he waved the gun in her face, and tightened the grip on her hair until she cried out. "Come on, Nina. Don't play games with me. I know Keel's contacted you. I followed him here the other night."

Nina was silent, realizing she hadn't felt this terrified in years. "Leave me out of this."

"Believe me," he said roughly, "if I could I would."

At that moment, she almost believed him.

"You did Keel a very big favor the last time you were in our town, Nina. You might even say you got him where he is today."

At the callous reminder, she went cold. "Stop it."

"He helped you, Nina. And now you're probably helping him."

She changed the subject, telling the only thing she knew. "Stan's dead."

Joe paused. His face, already grim, turned to granite.

"I swear to God he is." She began to panic at the rage she saw building there.

"How?" he demanded in a flat, unemotional voice.

Some of her panic subsided. Joe wasn't a killer... or was he?

"How, I said!" he demanded roughly.

She shivered. "He was hit on the head and he drowned when he fell into the lagoon on one of the rides. I'm sorry, Joe."

But he didn't move, didn't speak. She found the silence more chilling than the brutality.

She knew she had only one way out, and that was to deflect his interest from her, to get Joe to concentrate on someone else. Wetting her lips, she urged nervously, "Craig can help you, Joe."

At that he swore mightily.

She tried again. "If only you'd quit stabbing him in the back."

Joe checked the chamber of her gun, and found it loaded. He snapped it shut. "You forget, Nina. I know where that man's priorities are. And all he's been doing is trying to get rid of me for years. I don't trust him any more than he trusts me. And I sure as hell am not going to turn myself in. Watch your back, Nina. I'm gonna be watching mine."

And then he was gone.

With her gun in his hand.

Nina waited only thirty seconds, and then she put through a call to Commander Craig Keel.

IT WAS AFTER THREE O'CLOCK when Marianne woke to the faint but persistent sound of her smoke alarm in the living room. Exhausted, disoriented, she struggled to sit up.

Suddenly the alarm shut off.

Marianne listened, but heard only a faint crackling sound.

Panic thrumming in her veins, she leaped out of bed and snatched up her robe. Throwing it on, she dashed into the living room. The room was dark but she could see the thick smoke. Her panic intensified as she realized the apartment was on fire.

Coughing and choking, she schooled herself to remain calm as she made her way briskly to the front door. Her eyes tearing and burning, she knelt as she'd been taught to do and felt the bottom of the front door. It wasn't hot, which mean the fire wasn't out in the hall. Marianne sighed her relief and struggled to her feet.

She hadn't even reached the chain when she was grabbed and roughly shoved up against the door. There was a man in a gas mask standing in front of her. He was taller than she, dressed in heavy clothing, the kind firemen wore. "Where is the photo?" he demanded, his voice distorted behind the mask.

It was true what they said, she did see her life flash before her. Unable to scream because of the gloved hand over her mouth, sure she was going to die of smoke inhalation, she began to struggle. She might die, but it wouldn't be meekly.

Hands clawing for the door, she fought to get the dead bolt turned. He grabbed her again, a brutal hand on the back of her neck. Tightening his hold on her throat until she thought she would faint from lack of oxygen, he yanked her cruelly toward the kitchen. Her eyes widened with terror as she saw the fire leaping from the sink. She started to scream, inhaling a lungful of smoke. The burning was far worse than any pain her intruder could have inflicted.

"The picture," he demanded, pushing her face toward the dancing flames. "Where is the picture?"

Sanity and calm returned. She had to stall for time, pretend it was here, in the apartment.

"Over there." She pointed in the direction of the junk drawer where she kept various papers and photos and odds and ends and, at the very back, a sharp pair of kitchen shears.

Still holding onto her hair, he pushed her toward the drawer. He yanked it open, so everything went flying. In the firelight, they could both see the stack of old photos clearly. He pushed her down toward the drawer, and she knew what the heavy clothing he was wearing was—asbestos.

She felt herself getting weaker. She scrambled among the photos until her hand touched the shears. Adrenaline coursing through her veins, she turned and slashed out at his leg, cutting through the fabric, into his leg. He swore and lunged back, his voice distorted, loud, furious behind the mask. She slashed out again, this time higher. He backhanded her across the floor.

She saw him pick up the shears and come toward her furiously, while behind her the leaping flames spread ever upward to the cabinets, to the ceiling. She screamed then, loud and clear, not caring what the effort did to her lungs.

And then the fire alarm in the building began to sound.

THE CYPRESS CITY POLICEMAN was only the first of many to lecture her later. "If you were smart, Ms. Spencer, you'd stay out of police business and leave the investigating to us."

"Yeah, well, you know what they say, saved by the bell," Marianne gasped hoarsely as the paramedics continued to check her over.

"He's right," Bryant added seriously. Having heard the report of the fire on the police-band radio at the local FBI office, he'd been one of the first to arrive. "If you'd given up that photograph you wouldn't have been in any danger."

"If I hadn't taken it in the first place, I wouldn't have been in any danger," she corrected.

"I wish you'd give it to me now," he said, sighing. Although still the quintessential FBI agent, with the short layered haircut, the preppy suit and tie and white shirt, he also looked haggard and concerned and ten times more worried than he had earlier in the evening. Marianne was beginning to see why Pam and Seth trusted him so much.

Watching Bryant fuss over her, Doug looked a little bit jealous. He, too, had driven over immediately—but not because of the police. No, it had been Marianne who'd called him to come over. She'd needed him. And wise or not, she was going to be with him.

Doug laced a protective arm around Marianne's shoulders as she and Bryant continued to argue over the photo.

"I can't give it to you," Marianne said. If someone had gone to all this trouble to find it, it must be very valuable.

"For cripe's sake, why not?" Bryant demanded irritably.

"Because I don't have it," she said just as irritably, pushing the oxygen mask away. She looked at Bryant's face, saw he was determined to keep pushing her and decided impulsively on a lie. Anything to get him off her back. "Well, I can't help it. He burned it," she said defensively.

Bryant looked incredulous, then angry. "Who?"

Doug stood next to her, his face expressionless, as she continued, telling Bryant who'd stolen it. "The firebug, of course! It was in the stack of papers he used to start that fire in my kitchen. Stop looking at me like that! In the middle of a stack of week-old newspapers seemed like a very safe place to hide it until I could move it to my safety deposit box."

Bryant swore, and, finally believing her, turned and looked at Doug. "Do me a favor and keep an eye on her," Bryant said gruffly before stalking off.

Doug put the blanket around her shoulders. "Feeling better?"

Marianne took a few more gulps of oxygen, then took the mask off again, this time for good. "I just want to go home," she said tiredly.

He cast her a funny look. "I don't think it's inhabitable right now."

She shrugged, not caring where she crashed, as long as she could get some rest. "The fire's out."

"Yeah, and your kitchen is trashed." Fortunately, the rest of her building was intact. "How about my room? There's an extra double bed."

She looked at him carefully. "You wouldn't mind having me there?"

He smiled softly at her. "I couldn't sleep if you were anywhere else. Besides," he said, helping her into his rental car, "I want to go over the description of the man who attacked you one more time."

"OKAY, WE HAVE TALLER THAN YOU—maybe five ten or eleven, strong, with asbestos clothing and a gas mask."

"And a hat, now that I think about it," Marianne said, "or something on his head, because I don't ever remember seeing his hair."

"And that's it?"

"Doug, I was panicked. I didn't stop to make mental descriptions."

"I'm sorry. I just want to know who it was."

"So you can go after him?"

"Yes." He was serious.

"Doug—"

"I'm sorry," he apologized again. "It's been a rough night." His mouth was set in two white lines. His eyes were grim and protective. "Maybe we should get some sleep."

Now that was going to be next to impossible. She still smelled like smoke. And smoke made her remember. She shuddered, fighting back the sound of that distorted face behind the mask.

"Doug, would you mind if I took a shower?"

He took in her torn shirt, the filthy robe, the blanket donated to her by one of the neighbors. "Sure. Of course. Absolutely." He sprang into action. Five in the morning, the rest of the hotel was quiet. He came back thirty seconds later. "Everything's all set. I've got shampoo and soap and towels in there for you."

Everything she needed except one thing. "Doug, I need something to wear. I don't suppose you have any pajamas."

"I don't wear them. But maybe I can borrow something from Pam."

"No, don't bother her," Marianne said hurriedly.

"It's no problem," Doug soothed. "I'm sure she wouldn't mind."

He was gone before she could say anything, and back short minutes later, something white and silky crumpled up in his hand. "Uh, Pam's a light packer. She only brought two nightgowns. And they're both—well, you can see for yourself."

The bodice was sheer white lace, completely transparent, with spaghetti straps. The white skirt was slit from ankle to thigh up each side. "Sorry," he said.

"Yeah. Well..."

"Maybe one of my shirts would be better," he said. He strode over to his suitcase and returned with a Hawaiian print shirt that buttoned down the front.

"Thanks." Alone, neither garment would work to give her much modesty, but together, they just might do.

Abruptly, he looked as if he felt awkward, too. "I'll wait out on the balcony," he said quietly.

It took twenty minutes and several scrubbings before Marianne got the scent of smoke from her skin and hair. She toweled herself dry, then slipped on the nightgown and buttoned the shirt over that. When she walked back into the room, she could see Doug's figure silhouetted against the ever-lightening gray of the morning sky. Wanting company, she slipped out to join him.

He glanced at her makeshift attire. "Going to start a trend there," he remarked facetiously.

"Tell me about it."

They smiled. It was almost humorous, her ending up here with him.

"Ready to hit the sack?"

"Yeah."

They slid into separate beds. Marianne closed her eyes, then opened them again. Her breath caught in her throat. Panic oozed from her every pore.

"What's the matter?" he asked compassionately.

For a second she was too terrified to speak. To her embarrassment she felt sudden hot tears sting her eyes. She hadn't cried earlier. Why get emotional now?

He slid out of his bed and over onto hers. One arm slid beneath her shoulders. "What is it?" he said gently.

She took a rasping breath. "I saw the mask again."

Doug was silent for a minute. "Don't think about it."

She took another halting breath. She couldn't stop the shiver that ghosted down her spine. "I don't want to." Her hands felt icy, too.

"Close your eyes," he encouraged softly. "I'll stay with you."

She tried to do as he said, to go to sleep, but every time she shut her eyes, she opened them again just as swiftly. Finally, irritated with herself for behaving like a fool, she pushed out of his arms and from the bed. So she wouldn't sleep; so what? Anything was better than just lying there, waiting for the memories of her terror to resurface.

He let her get as far as the doors to the balcony before he caught up with her. "You've got to get some rest, after all you've been through."

"I can't."

"Yes, dammit, you have to."

Later, she was never quite sure how it had happened. One minute they'd been arguing, her head tilted up to his. The next they were kissing. Not the careful, gentle kisses of their early courtship, but fierce, hungry, demanding ones. Kisses that robbed her of the breath and will to think.

He gave her no chance to wonder or debate. Perhaps because of what she'd just been through, she understood there was no past or future, no present except for that moment. She arched into him, forgetting what she knew, what was practical, remembering only what she felt. Everything about her was wanting and yearning and hoping. She knew she needed to forget, she needed to feel, and perhaps he did, too.

He answered her every plea, her every wish, with hands that were as gentle as summer rain and the whispering wind, with kisses that were comforting and evocative, soulful and sweet. He seduced, he took, he gave, and she returned everything he gave her with everything she had, touching him the way he wanted to be touched, kissing him the way he wanted to be kissed.

They fell onto the nearest bed and found a comfortable niche in the tangled blankets.

Marianne hadn't known until now that lovemaking could bring on such wild waves of pleasure, such abandonment. She hadn't known what it meant to be truly vulnerable to another, to be part of his soul, his very existence, or to feel him a part of hers. She held him closer, closer still, until the world fell away, until they were on the edge, their hunger for one another strong and invincible, until they were tumbling head over heels into ecstasy, into love.

## Chapter Thirteen

*I promised myself I wasn't going to do this.* Marianne stood in the entrance to the nightclub. *I promised myself I wouldn't get any deeper involved with him than I already am.* But Doug was already on stage, and the music from his trumpet was floating over the audience, holding them mesmerized.

It took all of two seconds for Marianne to be drawn into his spell. Because the club was packed, she had to be content to stand along the far wall. She didn't mind; somehow just listening to Doug play was sensual pleasure in itself.

She'd taken piano, of course, and enjoyed it, had even been accompanist for the choir in high school. But what she'd done had never been like this. For a moment she envied Doug his ability to lose himself entirely in the music.

It was a gift, what he had. And knowing this, having heard him play, she hadn't been able to stay away. Not that night. Not after having made love with him and having spent the previous night sleeping in his arms. She was beginning to count on him, beginning to need him, and she knew, even if she didn't want to acknowledge it, that the whole situation was impossible. If she let herself make love with him even one more time, she would never get over the loss when he left. So what she had to do, she resolved, taking a deep breath, was end the love affair here and now. Maybe they could still be friends.

The set came to an end amid thundering applause. Doug lifted his head and smiled at the audience in recognition, then lifting his hand in a careless wave, slipped off the stage.

He was at her side in less than two seconds, his eyes traveling leisurely down her uniform. "Hi."

"Hi." She had thought by coming at the beginning of his performance she wouldn't have to confront him, that she would be able to get in and get out and just let things be. But then maybe this confrontation was destined, too. Maybe there were things that had to be said now, whether she liked it or not.

He picked up on her confused mood and his eyes darkened. At that moment he looked as scared and vulnerable as she felt. But when he spoke his voice was as commanding as always. "Come backstage with me." Not giving her a chance to say no, he took her hand in his, and threaded his way through the crowd.

"I didn't expect you to be here tonight," he said, sitting on the edge of his dressing table and drawing her in, to stand between his legs.

"I—" *Couldn't stay away* was on the tip of her tongue. But not wanting him to know how deeply enamored she was of him, she said lamely, "I wanted to hear you play again." *One more time.*

She'd wanted him to be horrible, so she could ask him to quit his job and stay on in Florida. He hadn't been. In fact, he'd been even more wonderful tonight than the first night at the Starlight Lounge.

Marianne glanced down at her hand. The nightclub had been lit only by candlelight on every table and she'd been able to hide in the shadows. Here, in the bright fluorescent lighting, she felt exposed and very vulnerable. Doug could see too much. He could see the yearning to be with him, the equally strong common sense that told her to run. She moved away from him, then watched as he put his trumpet gently back in the case.

Sighing with fatigue, he went over to the small refrigerator next to the dressing table and pulled out a bottle of Gatorade.

"I've got two sets left," he said after he'd drained half the bottle. "Want to wait for me?" His eyes held hers, telling her everything that was in his heart.

"I can't," Marianne said taking a deep breath and heading for the door. It was too much of a trial just being there with him. The sooner she left, the better. "I've got a lot of work waiting for me back at the office. My boss has been in a terrible mood."

"The photo—"

Marianne sighed. "It's still in the restaurant safe. I didn't get a chance to move it today. Don't worry, it's safe there."

He sighed, relenting. "I guess you're right."

Glancing at his watch, he finished the rest of his Gatorade, then tossed the empty bottle in the trash. "I've got to go back out there." He sighed and shot her a meaningful look, one that said he wanted her to stay.

"I'll see you tomorrow then."

He watched her, but said nothing.

It was all she could do not to touch him or kiss him. "You were wonderful," Marianne said with forced casualness. Even if she couldn't be with him, she wanted him to know how much she admired his talent.

"Thanks," he said shortly, his eyes holding hers. Disappointment was etched in the lines of his face as he picked up his trumpet again and headed for the stage. "But that's not what I want to hear from you, and you know it."

DOUG'S WORDS ECHOED in her head incessantly over the next few hours, through the time she spent at the office, and later during the short drive home. She knew he'd seen through her act, that he sensed the depth of her feelings for him. She didn't know what to do about it. She'd never been one to wear her heart on her sleeve, yet that was exactly what she was doing.

Her doorbell rang shortly after midnight. Dressed in jeans and an old sweatshirt, Marianne was in the kitchen sorting out the last of the confusion. Maintenance workers had been trying hard to repair the fire damage, and although it would be a while before the kitchen was back to normal, the room was in much better shape.

She walked over to the viewer, saw Doug standing there. She knew it would be someone friendly. Nina had insisted Marianne have around-the-clock CWR security men guarding her apartment building until the danger passed. Needing very much to feel safe, Marianne had agreed.

She should have known he'd show up. What she hadn't expected was how glad she was to see him, despite everything. "Hi," she said softly, careful to keep her voice cool and impersonal.

"Hi." He looked at her steadily until she invited him in with a wave of her hand. She moved away from the door as he entered, shutting it behind him.

She suddenly felt very confused and at a loss for words.

For Doug no words were really necessary. His hands were sliding around her back, pulling her close. "I missed you tonight," he confessed softly, his lips brushing her hair.

"Doug—" The precaution was a husky whisper. Panic swelled in her heart. Was this what she wanted? And if she did let him make love to her, how would she ever find the strength and courage to walk away? Was that what he wanted? For her to go with him when the time came to leave?

"Stop running, Marianne," he whispered, his palms sliding beneath her sweatshirt, up the bare skin of her back. He drew her close, until her breasts were pressed against his chest. She could feel the rapid beating of his heart; it matched the frantic cadence of hers. She could feel his tension, the wariness, the need. In his eyes, she saw tenderness and an affection that would abide.

There was nothing easy or slow about their lovemaking. It was all fast and furious, tempestuous and wild. He demanded. She gave. She asked for everything. He created her dreams. Later, locked together in her bed, she knew that like it or not her life had changed since she'd met him. Suddenly, nothing seemed so simple. Nothing seemed . . . settled.

"What is it?" Doug asked when she'd withdrawn slightly from his embrace.

Marianne was silent, confused. How was it possible just a week had passed since she'd met him? She felt like she'd known him a lifetime. "I can't help but wonder where all this will lead."

"I don't think we should try to solve everything in one night. I'm asking you to be with me," he said softly, persuasively, sliding a hand under her chin so she had no choice but to look at him. ''Not tomorrow, or the next day after that, but now, this minute.''

Suddenly, the time to deny her feelings was gone. She knew this was what she wanted, that if she didn't allow herself to experience the wonder of his love she'd never forgive herself, she'd always wonder what might have happened if only she hadn't been so stubborn. And then she knew she was in love with him. And he was in love with her. As much as she wanted to deny that, she couldn't. Not any longer.

JOE STOOD IN THE SHADE, mopping the sweat as it ran down his brow. This was turning out to be one hell of a vacation. Probably the worst one he'd ever had in his life and at the same time, the most productive one. Finally, after years of nothingness, being ignored and shunted aside, he was becoming important again. And not just to the people in his department at the NIS. But to the Soviets as well.

Those bumbling KGB idiots. They'd done everything they could to terrify his family. But not anymore. Now Joe had the goods on them.

They would deal with him. They had to. Now they had no choice.

''YOU'RE WRONG, ALL WRONG.'' Doug paced the conference room restlessly, and turned to face Commander Keel and the CIA agent he'd brought with him to talk to the family.

Marianne had sat in on the meeting at Doug's invitation.

''No way is my father dealing with the KGB.'' Billy and Pamela seconded their brother's claim.

"What other explanation is there?" Keel shot back evenly. He hoped by divulging the accusation the family would relent and cooperate with him, possibly even lead him to Joe—if only out of sheer patriotic duty, or fear of prosecution. "Your father is hiding. Stan's dead. We searched their apartments in D.C. and found a series of notes written in some sort of code. That code had nothing to do with anything they were assigned at work—it did look like a record of a series of meetings in very suspect locations, at very odd times of the day and night. Meanwhile, we've got a severe ongoing breach of Navy security that just resulted in a top-secret reconnaissance plane being shot down by the Russians. On the surface, it wouldn't seem as if there's any way the two events could be connected. Joe and Stan didn't have anything to do with the security involving those planes or their missions. They did, however, have access to NIS computers, and that information is in there."

"You're building a case out of circumstantial bull," Billy shot back hotly. "It's all nonsense and you know it!"

"Is it?" Keel asked steadily. "Tell me, then, why Joe and Stan both turn up in Florida at the exact same time two known KGB are also somewhere on the CWR complex."

"People come here from all over the world to vacation," Marianne protested.

"Right," the CIA man said. "And what better place to pass documents for cash in a way that would provide maximum cover? Who's going to suspect anyone on a family vacation of dealing with the KGB?"

"What documents?" Pamela spoke up, her face ashen. She looked worriedly from one man to another.

Keel shrugged. "The only leak we know about for sure now is the one concerning the planes, but technically they could sell just about anything from the NIS they could get their hands on. Joe and Stan both had top security clearances. Maybe they found out about the proposed missions for the planes and knew how valuable that would be to the Russians." His voice took on a harder edge. "And maybe they just wanted money to retire on, more than they had coming to them in their pensions."

"And maybe they didn't." Billy was as furious as Doug. "My father wouldn't do such a thing!"

"Maybe he wouldn't have years ago," Keel shot back smoothly. "But we all know Joe was not happy with the way his career had stalled over the past ten years. If he'd taken those field assignments in the Middle East that we wanted him to, of course—"

"What are you talking about?" Doug interrupted.

"Your father had plenty of chances to move up, but it would have meant moving out of the country. He didn't want to do that. He wanted to be close to his family, available—" Keel nodded to Doug and Pam "—in case either you or your sister needed him. Billy, he felt, could take care of himself."

The lines around Doug's mouth were white. Keel had said Joe had never talked about his family; obviously that was a lie. And if he would lie about that, what else would he lie about?

"Look, just let us know if you hear from him," the CIA man advised as he and Keel left the conference room. "It could mean the difference between life and death."

Doug looked at them, not sure who to trust. Billy seemed to be in some kind of shock. Pamela and Seth were equally quiet and shaken. Dammit, it wasn't true, Doug thought furiously. His father wasn't a spy.

"I've got to talk to my dad, to warn him about Keel," Doug said, as he and Marianne walked back to her office. "If only I had some clue as to where he was staying."

Marianne shared his sense of urgency. "Well, there is that message he sent you. Maybe we should take another look at that envelope."

"Good idea."

They stopped by the safe deposit box on the way home. In a private room, with the security guard stationed just outside the door, they took another look at the copy of "Ain't Misbehavin'." As Marianne had feared, nothing new came to them immediately.

Doug scowled, looking at the pristine sheet of mass-produced music.

And then it came to Marianne. She practically jumped up and down for joy. The clue they had been looking for was in front of their noses all this time, and they just hadn't seen it.

"What?" Doug demanded, knowing by her grin she was on to something.

"The music. Look at it, Doug. It's new. Brand new."

Doug looked over at the other music they had pulled from the fat yellow envelope. "And everything else is yellowed with age."

"Right. Which means—"

"Either Dad brought this with him, in case he needed to send any more messages—"

"Or he bought it somewhere in the area."

"Let's check the music stores."

Doug and Marianne drove into Cypress City and began showing the photo of Joe around. The first three times were useless: no one had seen anyone fitting Joe's description, nor did they carry the piano and guitar version of "Ain't Misbehavin'" in sheet music. The fourth store, however, did carry the music. And, yes, their computer confirmed, they had sold said music earlier in the week—it had been a cash transaction. "Do you recognize this man?" Doug asked, showing the clerk the photo. "Was he here in the store?"

The clerk shook his head. "Sorry. No. He wasn't here."

"Can you remember anything about the person who was here?"

"Well—"

At that instant, another clerk came into the store. Caught up on what the others had uncovered, he broke into a wide grin. "Yeah, I was working that afternoon," he said. "Only it wasn't a man that bought that music, but a woman. Horn-rimmed glasses, kind of efficient-looking. You know her?"

"I sure do," Doug said grimly. It was his sister.

"WILL YOU STOP YELLING AT ME a minute? I was only trying to help!" Pam protested, an hour later.

"Look, Doug, it was my idea." Seth stepped in to protect his fiancée. "Pam was driving herself crazy, worrying you were going to get hurt playing super sleuth. It's not good for her, worrying so much—in her condition. So I figured if I sent you a message like the one Stan sent your dad, you'd listen, and cool it, and Pam could relax."

"It was a stupid thing to do!" Doug fumed.

"Doug, I'm sorry," Pamela said, her skin turning even more ashen.

"It won't happen again," Seth promised.

It had better not, Doug thought darkly. "Is there anything else you're not telling me?" he questioned impatiently. "Anything else you've told me that's a lie?"

Pam hesitated a fraction too long. Doug realized with a start his sister wasn't sharing everything she knew with him. Was it possible Joe had confided in her, and not his eldest son? And if so, did that make Doug even a bigger failure in his father's eyes?

"Pam?"

Seth stepped in. "Can't you see she's just over-wrought, Doug? I think she needs to rest. Honey, we don't want you getting sick again."

Pam looked relieved to have found an out. "You're right, we should calm down."

Doug scowled at them both, not sure what to believe. They both looked so innocent. He wanted to trust them. The question was, could he? Now suddenly he didn't know.

Pam and Seth left. Billy, who'd been quiet during most of the exchange—too quiet—was still looking troubled.

"What is it?" Doug asked.

Billy shook his head, as if that would help dispel his doubts. Finally, he admitted in a low, disturbed tone, "Pam and Seth aren't the only ones who're scared. I'm having my doubts, too, about Dad's innocence." He sucked in his breath at Doug's irate look, and hurried on. "Look, I don't want to think Dad would sell out, either. But look at things from his point of view. He was frustrated, about to retire—"

"Dad wouldn't sell out his country," Doug said firmly, knowing it in his gut. Then, knowing there was mote to Billy's mood than just tension, he said, "There's more, isn't there?"

Billy let out his breath slowly and nodded grimly. "Dad's quizzed me on the latest codes and missions the last couple of times we met. At the time I didn't think anything about it. We always talked freely to one another about Navy matters. I mean, if you can't trust your own father who can you trust?"

Doug felt sick inside, sick and scared. "What do you think this has to do with Keel?" he demanded.

"Well...you remember that plane that got shot down a couple days ago? There have been other incidents like it the past six months. No one has been able to figure out yet if they're just flukes, or if it is more than that."

The sick feeling in Doug's middle increased. "Espionage?"

Billy nodded unhappily. "Maybe. Anyway, what if Dad and Stan were trying to crack this thing? What if they stumbled onto more than they bargained for?"

"You think they're being set up to take a fall?"

Billy nodded. "At least that's what I want to believe."

Doug looked at his younger brother. He still seemed all torn up inside, unsure. Afraid. "You can't seriously think Dad would've willingly gotten involved in anything illegal, do you?"

Billy didn't answer for a long moment, and then he shrugged. "No," he said finally, "I guess not." But it was clear from the way he spoke the doubts were still there.

Doug, on the other hand, had no doubts. None at all. He believed in his father every bit as strongly as he ever had. He wondered if that made him the fool.

DOUG AND BILLY STARED FIXEDLY at the computer screen Tuesday evening, elated by what they'd just discovered. "What'd I tell you?" Billy crowed to the other members of the family in the room. "Hot damn!" He pushed a few more buttons with precise, mechanical motions. "I've broken it!"

Marianne edged nearer as Doug read the messages out loud. "Major complications. Meeting canceled. Do not go into park. Wait for further notice."

"So," Marianne theorized slowly, "Joe wasn't supposed to go into the park at all on Sunday."

"He wouldn't have, if he'd gotten the message in time," Doug agreed.

"But he didn't get the message and he did go into the park. And something went wrong from there," Marianne said.

Doug continued, "Something must have happened when he went to the arranged meeting. Something maybe Stan had already anticipated."

"You think there was trouble?" Marianne asked.

"Why else would he have run? Why else would Stan have told him not to go?" Doug asked.

"Unless maybe it was a trap of some sort," Marianne said, feeling as if she were standing in a dark closet and a light had suddenly gone on.

"But a trap set by whom?" Doug wanted to know.

"Hard to say." Billy shrugged.

Marianne agreed. "Could be anyone. The KGB themselves. The CIA. Even the NIS."

"If it were the KGB, it would explain Dad's running," Pam said quietly, a distant look in her eyes. "I know he'd do just about anything—even risk his own life—to keep his family safe."

"So what do we do in the meantime?" Billy asked.

"I don't think we should give it to Keel or Bryant or anyone else at this point," Doug said. "Not until we can figure out more clearly who is friend and who is foe."

Pam and Seth agreed, after a moment's deliberation between themselves. "We'll just have to trust that Dad can more than take care of himself," Pam said quietly. But she, like the others, still looked and felt scared.

"THANKS FOR INVITING ME out on the lake," Doug said half an hour later. Sensing Marianne and Doug wanted more time alone, Pam and Billy both had urged Doug to take a break for just a little while. They'd had another hour and a half before dark. So Marianne had made a quick call to the docks just outside his hotel room.

Doug had driven the speedboat out into the middle of the lake. From there, they were content to cut the engine and drift a while.

After spending the day cooped up inside, both appreciated the fresh air, and the chance to experience the sunset. In the distance, red streaked the horizon. The evening was still warm, almost unbearably so, but the breeze gently caressed their bodies and rippled through their hair.

Marianne reached over and took Doug's hand. "After all you've been through," she answered him calmly, "I felt like you needed a break."

He grinned, the depth of his fatigue showing around his eyes. "I do and I don't—know what I mean?" He stretched his broad shoulders lazily. "Mostly, I'd prefer the whole thing just to be over."

"Well, unfortunately, that I can't give you."

His hand tightened on hers, his thumb caressing her knuckles lightly. "I know. It's enough sometimes just knowing you're here for me."

"Are you okay otherwise?" she asked, when she sensed something was still bothering him.

"I feel like I'm walking on air, after being with you last night." His voice dropped a husky notch. "And at the same time, I'm worried about the future. I'm only supposed to be here ten days. I've already decided I'll stay until I get definite word on my dad, however long it takes. But even after that, I don't want to leave."

Those were the words she'd been waiting to hear. "Then don't," Marianne said, holding his eyes.

"What do you mean?"

"I have my work here."

"Live off your salary, you mean?" The suggestion was one he'd heard before and hated.

"Would that be so terrible?"

"Yes." His jaw assumed a stubborn tilt.

"I'm not talking forever," Marianne began emotionally, "just—"

"Until I figure out what I want to do?" The words were bitter.

"Right."

"Marianne," he said tiredly, releasing her hand, "I already know what I want to do with my life. I'm doing it." He now had the patience of a saint, and the reserve. She felt emotionally they were light years apart.

His distance hurt. Nonetheless, she knew she had to be honest with him, to say what was true, and not just what would bring peace.

But he cut her off briskly before she could speak. "You like your job, don't you?"

"It's taken me years to get where I am," she admitted, hearing defiance creep into her tone. Her spine stiffened. She'd be damned if she'd apologize for being successful, for being good at what she did. "Yes, I like it." Just as she loved him.

"You couldn't consider giving it up?"

"To do what and go where?"

He didn't have the answer; they both knew he lived on the road, out of hotels, and went wherever the next gig was, for however long. "Life's a bitch sometimes, isn't it?" he asked unhappily.

Marianne nodded wearily, feeling as if she had just aged about one hundred years. "You can say that again."

They were silent. The sun had dropped almost to the horizon.

Doug's arm hugged her shoulders. When she slanted him a glance, he was smiling. And somehow invincible in a very sexy way. "Well, I guess there's nothing left to do except enjoy what we have."

His mood was catching. She found herself smiling back even as her troubled thoughts rambled on. The next few days. Would it be enough? She discovered it would have to be because she wasn't letting him go before she absolutely had to, and maybe even then... Maybe if they just slept on it, gave it time, a solution would present itself. She had to hope so, anyway.

"Maybe we should just take it one day at a time, for a few days longer," she suggested finally.

"I'm all for that." He bent and kissed her soundly.

Doug didn't kiss like a man who was preparing to leave her, she thought, but rather like a man who couldn't walk away.

It would work out. It had to.

## Chapter Fourteen

"All right, we'll go through it one more time," Craig Keel snarled irritably early Wednesday morning. They'd been at this most of the night and, thanks to the noncompliance of his subordinate, were getting nowhere fast. Joe hadn't told them anything since CWR Security had picked him up after the park closed, prowling around Liberty Hall in the International Bazaar. He hadn't been carrying any ID on him, but a quick-witted security officer had recognized Joe from the pictures Marianne circulated, and called Nina, who had in turn called him. Craig had met them all at the Cypress City police station. "What are you doing in Florida?"

Joe shrugged noncommittally. "Vacationing with my family."

"Your family hasn't seen you since the day you arrived."

Joe grinned uncooperatively, his attitude belligerent. "Then I'll have to make more time for us to spend together."

Keel scowled at Joe, not liking his smart attitude one bit. He was making Keel look bad. "Why was Stan here?" Keel asked, in a clipped tone of voice.

"I don't know." Joe shrugged. "I guess he felt he deserved a vacation, too."

"You're not helping yourself, Joe."

Joe's eyes narrowed. "I'm not helping you, either."

"Be reasonable—"

"No, you be reasonable, *sir*." Forgetting his station, Joe stood, and thumped Keel on the chest with the point of his extended index finger. "For the past five years you couldn't have cared less what Stan or I thought about anything. You didn't trust us to be able to handle anything remotely sensitive. You put us aside and on a shelf like forgotten rag dolls. And now you want me to trust you? To tell you my deepest, darkest secrets?" Joe sat back down before the MPs could assist him. "Forget it," he snarled.

"Joe," Bryant Rockwell tactfully intervened. "The commander is only trying to help."

"Yeah, sure." Joe glared straight ahead.

"We need to know what's been going on," Bryant continued soothingly.

Joe sent him a fierce look. "I can't help you."

Keel and Bryant exchanged frustrated looks.

Bryant was the first to speak. His tone was grim. "Then you better get yourself a good lawyer, Joe. Because you're sure as hell going to need one."

"HE WON'T COOPERATE in the slightest," Bryant informed Doug as soon as he arrived at the Cypress City jail where Joe was being detained.

"Somehow that doesn't surprise me."

"Well, see what you can do," Bryant urged. "If he doesn't trust Keel, I understand. But he's got to confide in some of us if we hope to ever have a chance of straightening this thing out."

"I'll do what I can," Doug assured Bryant. He could see he was falling all over himself trying to help.

Doug's feelings changed the moment he walked into the cell. His dad looked like he'd been through hell: he had shadows beneath his eyes, and he'd lost weight. Doug had to choke back a knot of emotion in his throat. After all the days of not knowing, it was good just to see him alive. But he was angry, too; his dad didn't belong behind bars and it hurt seeing him there. He was also resentful his father hadn't contacted him during the crisis; he had to have known what hell they'd all been through.

Joe read the confusion in his son's expression, and his face softened understandingly. Not saying a word, he walked forward to give his son a hard hug. Doug felt the love in that hard embrace. He knew then, instinctively, that whatever his father had done, he'd had no choice.

"Everything all right?" Joe asked hoarsely. "With your sister and brother? Seth?"

Doug took a deep breath, fighting back his own tears of relief. "Everything's fine."

There was so much to say, and virtually no privacy. Doug felt a renewed sense of anger. No matter what had transpired, his father didn't deserve to be treated like a common criminal.

He looked at his father, seeking reassurance himself. There seemed to be so much going on with him, and yet so little he could say. They sat down on the narrow metal bunk, aware a Navy guard and a Cypress City police officer stood several feet away, listening avidly to everything that was being said. "Dad, why did you go underground?"

"I had to."

"Why?"

"Everything was complicated. I knew I was in jeopardy and I figured if I was with you, or you even knew how to find me, that you would be, too."

"Who's after you?"

"It doesn't matter."

"It does to me."

"Listen to me, Doug. Leave it alone."

"I can't."

Doug knew he wouldn't get anywhere with his father by trying to reason with him. Could he scare him into cooperating? "You know about Stan," he said slowly.

Joe nodded reluctantly, a look of sorrow moving over his face. "I was told. But when I didn't hear from him, I figured."

"Did someone try to kill you, too?"

Joe said nothing.

"Do you know who killed him?" Doug persisted, getting frustrated with his father's reticence. Now he was in custody, why wouldn't he let anyone else help him?

Joe cast a cautionary look at the guard and, avoiding the question, concentrated on confirming the specific details of his friend's death. "He drowned, didn't he?"

Doug nodded slowly, wondering what his father was getting at, how much he really knew. "Yeah. At least that's my understanding," he said slowly. "Dad, he was drugged." Doug emphasized the words calmly.

"So Keel said."

"With truth serum. Nobody can figure out what he knew that would've been so important—"

Without warning, Joe broke down and began to sob. Doug stared at his dad, not knowing what to do. His father had never collapsed emotionally in his life, not even when his mother had died. He was the coolest, most self-contained person he knew.

Doug cast a disparaging glance at the Navy personnel standing off to one side of the corridor and then moved to take his dad into his arms. His father continued to sob, his shoulders shaking with the effort. And then he whispered, so only Doug could hear. "Was Stan carrying anything on him when he died?"

So, it was all an act, Doug thought, relieved. "No," he said out loud, for benefit of those witnesses, "it's not your fault." Whispering, Doug continued, "There was nothing on him."

"Then he probably dumped it somewhere close to where he died," Joe continued to whisper, between loud sobs. "It's in a Wacky Duck doll, Doug," he said secretively. "Find it Doug. Find it and destroy it."

"WHERE WOULD YOU HIDE a Wacky Duck doll?" Doug wondered softly as he and Marianne slowly circled the 20,000 Leagues ride.

"There were several trash cans nearby. Maybe he tossed it in one of them," Marianne theorized. "Especially if it were going to be destroyed anyway."

"No. That was too risky," Doug decided. "Stan was a cautious man, a thinker. He wouldn't have acted so rashly. What if the KGB saw him toss it? They'd pick it up and that would be it." He frowned, studying the map. "There's a men's room not too far from here."

"Well, there's a waste can there. It's emptied every couple of hours. It'd be impossible to flush a stuffed animal without backing up the commodes."

"Which you would have heard about."

"You're not kidding."

Doug turned to study the exterior of the ride. A six-foot chain-link metal fence was hidden by towering shrubs and a profusion of flowers. They knew from the cuts on Stan's hands that he had jumped over the fence, probably under cover of darkness, since an action like that would be too conspicuous in the daylight. From there, he had probably crouched among the many bushes disguising the other side of the fence.

"It wasn't in the water."

"If it had been, the divers would have found it."

"Which means he would've had to hide it somewhere in the landscaping." Marianne said.

"We hope." Doug sighed. He knew his dad was counting on him to come up with the duck and destroy it. He knew the duck—or whatever was in it—had cost Stan his life. He glanced around as casually as possible. "Can we go in there, in the rocky area surrounding the ride, and look around?"

"Not during park hours. Not without attracting a lot of attention," Marianne whispered. "But maybe when the park closes. I'll have to get special permission from the head of horticulture."

"All right." Doug got out the map of the Enchanted Village and pretended to study it again. Marianne moved closer to him, wondering what he was looking at. "Keel had us tailed," Doug reported, under his breath.

"Who?"

"The guys in the blue and green shirts."

Marianne smiled. "Want to lose them?"

Doug smiled, too, his eyes holding hers. How had he ever gotten along without her? "Would you mind?" he said softly, bending to give her a tender kiss.

Marianne shook her head and signaled for her own two men in CWR security uniforms. "Not a bit."

Two and half minutes later, Doug was a free man. Or as free as he was likely to get.

THE CHIEF SECURITY OFFICER was waiting for her when Marianne returned to her office. He looked anxious and upset, so Marianne shut her door, to ensure their privacy. "You know that other guy you asked us to tail— Tom Merchant?"

"Right. The one who had his camera stolen."

"He met a couple of foreigners on Adventure Island at two-thirty this afternoon. I know they were foreigners because they were speaking some other language when they thought they were alone."

"What language?"

"I'm no expert, but it sounded to me like Russian."

Marianne drew in a quick breath as the revelation sunk in. Were they dealing with the KGB. "What did they look like?"

"One was kind of swarthy, with dark, thinning hair, the other was tall and blond, a real cold one, that guy."

"Was Mr. Merchant being threatened?"

"No, ma'am. At least not from where my man stood. The three of them looked thick as thieves."

That was a puzzle, Marianne thought. If these were the same men who'd stolen Tom's camera, and it sounded as if they were, why would he be meeting with them now? Unless he'd been involved with them all along.

That possibility presented several questions and worries.

"And now for the bad news." The security chief sighed, seeing her dismay. "My man lost them as soon as they left the island. I guess they realized they were being followed."

Marianne frowned, disappointed and a little scared. "So now no one knows where Tom Merchant is."

"No, ma'am. They don't. But the good news is he doesn't appear to be in any danger—at least not from those two foreigners who allegedly stole his camera."

"Did he get his camera back from them?"

"No. As far as I saw, nothing at all changed hands. They just stood there and talked for a few minutes, then split up again." He paused. "Do you think this might be some sort of an insurance racket? You did mention the camera was an expensive one—"

It was some kind of racket, all right, Marianne thought. She just wasn't sure what kind.

"WHERE ARE YOU GOING?" Nina Granger asked, as Marianne headed out the door. Damn, Marianne thought, she would have to run into Nina now, just when she was finally getting somewhere. Nor had she been able to find Doug, who was probably out still scouting around the Enchanted Village, trying to find hiding places for the Wacky Duck doll.

Marianne knew regret would come later, but for now she had to act and get rid of Nina. "We had some VIPs come in, a senator from Washington State and his family," Marianne lied. "I thought I'd run by the gift shop, pick up a complimentary basket of fruit and take it by their room."

Nina smiled, able to find no fault with that. "Oh. Good idea. Anything new on the Maitland situation?"

"Well, yes and no," Marianne said evasively. "I guess you heard Joe Maitland was located somewhere on the grounds last night, trying to break into an apartment, and taken in to Cypress City jail for questioning earlier this morning.''

"No," Nina said calmly, "I didn't know that. But then I just got in to the office myself. I was working at home this morning."

Marianne nodded, not caring where Nina had been or why. If only she could get rid of her as easily now. "Well, he was put in jail. He's being held for questioning. His son Doug was pretty upset about it—"

"I can imagine." Nina regarded Marianne steadily as she reached into her pocket for a pack of cigarettes.

With effort, Marianne kept her voice unperturbedly even. "But they haven't pressed any charges against him yet, so I guess everything will work out."

Nina relaxed slightly. "I hope so," she said, flicking her lighter on. "CWR doesn't need any bad press."

No, it didn't. But that wasn't Marianne's main concern. Not any more.

Excusing herself politely, she hurried toward the gift shop. She picked up what she needed, then stopped at a pay phone to ring Tom Merchant's room. No answer. Replacing the receiver, Marianne thought, *Here goes.*

She used her pass key to get into Tom's room. It was empty, as she had hoped, the drapes drawn against the sunlight. Putting the basket of fruit and the welcoming card from CWR in a prominent place, she began to quickly search the room. The bureau drawers were empty. His suitcases were closed but unlocked. Rummaging through them carefully, Marianne found nothing irregular.

The closet held two business suits, and several starched white cotton shirts. There was also a tripod— she supposed for the camera he'd lost.

The bathroom was a complete mess. Wet towels on the floor, soap and shaving gear out. *Wait just a minute....*

Shaving gear? The man had a beard—or he had one the last time Marianne had seen him. And yet there were flecks of shaving foam and facial hair in the sink.

Really curious now, she looked in the small zippered travel bag. There were several tubes of facial adhesive, toothpaste, deodorant, a bottle of after-shave, a small container of rice powder. Gingerly, she uncapped the bottle and took a whiff. The musky familiar smell sent her reeling.

She put it aside, her fingers shaking. There was no doubt in her mind this was the scent worn by the man who'd broken into her apartment and left her tied up.

He was the burglar. He was working with the KGB.

Oh, God, she had to get out of there. And fast.

Moving quickly, she put everything back exactly as she had found it and slipped out of the room, locking the door behind her.

She borrowed the office and phone of a hotel colleague for expediency's sake. Running a quick financial check on Mr. Tom Merchant, she soon discovered he had been paying for his room with his bank credit card issued in his name, out of the First City Bank in Chicago, and he was very near his credit limit of six thousand dollars.

"I'm concerned about his being able to pay for his stay here at Children's World," Marianne said, using a confidential tone.

The bank loan officer was not pleased to hear that. "How much of a tab has he run up?"

"Close to one thousand dollars."

"You should have called us sooner."

Marianne let dread creep into her tone. "You mean I'm dealing with a deadbeat?"

"I'm sorry, but he's already passed his credit limit. We can't okay anymore charges."

"Is there any chance he can get an immediate emergency credit hike from your bank?"

"No way." The loan officer was firm about this much.

Which meant he had a bad history with them, no doubt. Marianne sighed, trying to extract all the information she could. "I don't understand. He seems like such a nice man. On the surface, anyway." Again, there was no response from the person on the other end of the line. "I have to decide whether or not to allow him to continue to stay here."

There was a sigh on the other end of the line. "Look, I don't know what to tell you. Maybe the guy has another card, or can get a line of credit at another bank."

"Maybe," Marianne replied evenly, knowing she'd pushed her luck as far as possible. "Listen, thanks for all your time and the information."

"No problem."

But it was a problem, Marianne thought, hanging up the phone. It was her problem. Because whatever was going on, Tom Merchant was somehow at the center of it now. And maybe he had been all along.

ACROSS THE PARK, there was trouble, too. "Will you watch where you're going?" Seth hissed as Pam tripped over a rock.

"I'm trying! And stop following me so closely. You're making me nervous."

"I can't help it." Seth shuddered. "This island gives me the creeps."

"Make that two of us," Pamela muttered. She was nauseated and tired, and couldn't wait for this all to be over.

She took the Misty Mouse doll from her carryall and set it low, next to a tree trunk, as she'd been instructed to do.

Seth, still glancing around them paranoidly, kept his body between the path and Pam. Overhead, the birds chattered incessantly. He wished he'd had a gun, but maybe that wasn't so smart either, since he'd never used one.

He turned his attention back to the Misty Mouse doll. "Cover it up with some mulch," Seth instructed. "And tear up some of that grass and those ferns and put that around it, too. We don't want some tourist picking it up before those stupid, syringe-wielding barbarians arrive."

Pam turned toward him incredulously. "Are you kidding? Do you have any idea what kind of fines there are for tearing up the landscaping here?"

"Not half as costly as the ones those blackmailing barbarians'll impinge upon us if we screw up this drop, too," Seth muttered darkly.

Pam paled, looking at his bandaged hand. It didn't take much to make her remember Seth being held spread-eagled against the side of his car, the door slammed shut on his fingers and open palm. The excruciating pain he'd been in, the screams that had seemed to echo throughout the dark, nearly abandoned parking garage, the blood... No, she didn't want to go through that again, and she knew whatever the KGB did the next time would be much, much worse. They'd already promised as much.

THE SWARTHY MAN SWORE virulently under his breath. "We have searched every inch of this bloody island!"

"You're right. The drop isn't here," the thin man in the Coca-Cola shirt said.

"There's no stuffed duck, no mouse—"

"We've been lied to again."

"I will kill Merchant this time." The swarthy man pounded his fist on his palm.

"You will have to stand in line, comrade."

"Only if you get there first."

They stared at one another, their tempers frayed. This was their last chance, too. And they were both erring beyond measure. "Where is he?"

The thin spy shrugged. "I don't know." But when he found him . . . Yeah, he would suffer, and suffer badly!

"Perhaps his partner—" the swarthy man began, contemplating ways to finish off Merchant that would reap the most pain.

"Will lead us to him," the thin man finished, his confidence returning.

The swarthy man flashed an evil smile. "My thoughts . . . exactly."


Marianne drove quickly to the Seven Seas village, where the Maitlands were staying. Doug had promised to meet her there later, but she needed to talk to someone in the family now. If not him, then his sister, Pam, or brother, Billy. Someone close to Joe.

Unfortunately, there was no answer to her knocking. Using her passkey, she let herself into Billy's room. There was no clue as to where he'd gone.

Pam and Seth's room, however, was another matter. It, too, was devoid of people—with no clues left as to where the young couple had gone. But laid prominently out on the bed was a blond wig, sunglasses, a rather crumpled sunhat. Marianne stared at them, realizing full well that the woman Joe had been battling with the night he disappeared had been a blonde, wearing a hat and sunglasses.

Had that been Pam? The airline tickets and hotel vouchers Marianne had seen earlier in the week substantiated the fact Pam had been in Florida then—a full two and a half days before she was supposed to arrive.

Had Pam really been the woman in the park that night? Or was someone else just trying to falsely implicate her now, the way Marianne and Doug had been implicated—with the camera and microfilm and stacks of one-hundred-dollar bills? Was the whole family being framed? Or was his family really guilty?

If Pam were somehow mixed up in the investigating Joe was obviously doing, it would explain his refusal to talk to the authorities now. Especially if Pam were a target of the KGB. Marianne remembered how Pam had gotten sick directly after the KGB men had entered the Mexican restaurant that night. But they hadn't known who the two men were at that point. Bryant hadn't told them they were KGB until later.

But why and how would Pam have gotten mixed up with people like that in the first place? Marianne wondered. Was it for the money?

Was Seth involved, too? Had his hand been hurt in an accident, as Pam had stated, or had it been done deliberately, maybe by the same people who had tried to push Marianne's face into the flames? Was he in danger, too?

Had Pam and Seth cooperated with the KGB because they feared for their lives if they didn't?

Maybe Joe had been blackmailing the KGB, exactly as it appeared, to try to get them to leave his daughter alone.

Unhappily, Marianne had no one to go to with her questions. Not now. Impulsively, she took the clothes and the wig and the sunglasses and shoved them behind a stack of towels in the laundry room.

That accomplished, she set out to find Doug. She had to tell him what she knew.

"STOP POINTING THAT GUN at my back, would ya? You're making me nervous."

"Just make the call," the armed man said. "And do exactly as we say. No ad libs. Got it?"

"Don't get upset, buddy. I understand. Though what you'd want with her—"

"None of your business!" he said. "Just make the call."

The security guard was sweating profusely. He glanced at the clock on the wall. Eleven o'clock. His ride had already shut down for the night because of electrical problems.

Some electrical problems. He thought he had the source of the electrical problems breathing down his neck right now. But there wasn't much he could do except cooperate with the man with the gun. It was either that or get his head blown off. He had no doubt the man meant what he said.

Hand shaking, he picked up the phone and dialed guest relations. "Marianne Spencer please. What do you mean she's not in? Well, can I reach her? It's important. No. I can't talk to anyone but Ms. Spencer. Sure, I'll wait."

The man took the safety latch off the trigger. The click was audible in the darkness. "Don't screw up now," he warned darkly.

"Dammit," the guard muttered under his breath. "Yeah. Ms. Spencer? It's Carl Ondretti over at the Haunted House. You know that camera you were looking for earlier in the week? Well, I think I found it. We had electrical problems on the ride tonight. One of the crew was working on the track, trying to fix it, and he found the camera. It had fallen under a couple of chairs. Yeah, I've still got it. No, I haven't notified lost and found. I thought I'd call you first, since you were looking for it. Bring it there? Well, no, I can't. I've gotta—You'll come here? That's great. No. No problem. Right. I'll be waiting for you. As soon after midnight as you can make it."

The guard hung up the phone and turned to his accoster. "Done. Exactly as you wrote it." He was still sweating. "You gonna kill me?" he asked, wishing he'd been a little less careless in the use of his own weapon.

"That all depends on what kind of job you do next." The man smiled. "In the meantime, we'll just sit here and wait—for the real fun to begin."

## Chapter Fifteen

"What are you still doing here this time of night?" Nina Granger asked Marianne just outside her office.

"Trying to catch up on a few loose ends."

"Any luck?"

*Yes. In fact an incredible lot,* Marianne thought. "Uh, no."

Nina was still blocking her way. "Anything new on Joe Maitland?"

"Not that I've heard. Although I talked to Billy a while ago. He's still at the jail with his father, and intends to stay there all night."

"Is Joe confiding in him?"

"No, but Billy is determined to get him to cooperate, and if anyone can, it's him."

"How's the rest of the family taking it?" Nina asked sympathetically.

Marianne stared at Nina. She'd rarely known her to be this concerned about anyone else. It was as if in some ways she'd gone through a metamorphosis, too, the past couple of days. "They're understandably upset," Marianne said cautiously. She was anxious to sign the papers that had to be signed and sent out in the morning mail, so she could run over to the Haunted House and pick up that camera.

"I guess so."

"Any luck finding out where the suspected spies were housed?"

About that, Marianne sighed her disappointment. She and Bryant had talked to every reservations clerk in the area, showed them the picture. None remembered seeing the thin blond KGB agent check in. "Uh, no," Marianne admitted, still restless. "You?"

Nina shrugged, looking innocent but uncomfortable. "Commander Keel said they haven't found a thing. Marianne, you're sure everything's okay? You're looking very strange."

She felt strange and excited. And somewhat scared. "It's just been a long day," Marianne replied, finishing up her paperwork. She stifled a fake yawn. "I think I'll go home."

Nina nodded slowly, still watching her carefully. "Maybe that would be best."

On that note, Marianne rushed out of her office. Nina stared after her, knowing Marianne wasn't going home. Nina had lived with fear long enough to know it, and she knew Marianne well enough to tell when she was excited.

Clearly, Marianne thought she'd found the breakthrough she had been looking for. So what? This was none of her business. If Nina were smart, she would stay out of it because she knew full well how much heartache could come from getting involved. Once before, when she'd been in her early thirties, she'd been confident she could manage anything, too.

A fast-track executive with an east-coast management corporation that managed huge condominium complexes, Nina had been in charge of the vast D.C. operation. It was her first big project, and at first, everything had gone smoothly. Then she had noticed some shady dealings between some Oklahoma oilmen and some Arabs. She had turned to Craig Keel, a Navy officer and neighbor she trusted. With her help, and some major investigating on both their parts, they had eventually uncovered a plot to blow up some oil rigs in the Persian Gulf. The proof they garnered had been enough to send some very angry men to prison. Craig had been on his way, careerwise. And because the Arabs had feared military men and retaliation, he had been relatively safe from recriminations. Nina then became the sole target of the already crazy woman-hating Arab group. She'd seen her car blown up, her best friend right along with it. After that, she'd been given a new identity. The U.S. government had helped change her looks. They'd gotten her a job at Children's World.

Life had gone on, if not as happily as before, at least as smoothly and much more quietly. She'd had no problems since.

But now the anonymity she had struggled for was threatened. A scandal at Children's World would make them all front-page news, worldwide. There was a chance she might be photographed and then recognized by someone in the media. If that happened, she'd have to move on again. She'd worry about the same group of people who'd been after her before coming after her again. She didn't want to start living her life in fear again. And the thought of tangling with the KGB made her very nervous. It reminded her too much of the ruthlessness of the Arab extremists.

All she had to do was stay out of it, trust Marianne to be able to handle whatever happened.

Maybe Marianne could.

But what if she couldn't?

Could Nina live with that?

MARIANNE DROVE THE CART rapidly over to the Enchanted Village. She still hadn't heard from Doug, although she'd solved that problem by leaving a message for him with the doorman in her building. If Doug came in, he'd be told where she went, and he could meet her there.

Her pulse raced frantically as she drove her cart through the employees' gate. She stopped to sign in at the guardhouse. It was an effort to keep her voice calm and steady; she felt breathless and excited. "Mr. Doug Maitland should be following me. If he comes in, would you ask him to meet me at the Haunted House?"

"Sure thing, Ms. Spencer. Would you like me to have him escorted there by one of the guards?"

Marianne shook her head. If she was on to something, she didn't want anyone else in on it until they had a chance to turn it over to the proper authorities, as well as a top-notch lawyer they could trust to work on Joe's behalf. "No. He knows the way. Just send him on back." It was past midnight and the Enchanted Village was now closed to the public. And since no one else knew where she was going, she would be safe. So why was she still so nervous?

From the Haunted House, they would head over to the 20,000 Leagues ride. She'd gotten permission to dig very gently in the landscaping surrounding the lagoon. With luck, before morning, they would have not just the answers they were seeking, but the evidence to support their claims as well.

The Haunted House was eerily dark when Marianne reached it, and she felt a moment's pause. Battling the sudden urge to turn and run, she schooled herself firmly to calm down. Of course the lights were out; that wasn't unusual. Cleaning crews weren't due to arrive until four in the morning. For the next three and a half hours the interior of the park would be barren, except for the skeleton crew of security men patrolling the area. Nothing was wrong. No one knew about the camera but her. Besides, she wasn't totally sure this was the camera Tom Merchant had lost. What if it wasn't? What if she was making much ado about nothing?

Parking her cart in front of the building, Marianne took a deep breath, squared her shoulders and started inside. There was no need for her knees to be quaking so, she thought, irritated with her unusually wimpish behavior. "Hello?" she called in a cheerful voice. "Mr. Ondretti? It's Marianne Spencer."

There was a gust of air behind her, the sound of soft sliding footsteps; a corresponding shiver of fear rippled through her body. And then the confirmation she'd been a terrible fool, that she'd just put her life in irrefutable danger. "Hello, Marianne Spencer." The deadly voice coincided with the metal rod digging painfully into her spine.

"Don't turn around," the low voice continued as the man jabbed her again, hard enough to leave a bruise. "Just keep walking. That's it." Her accoster grabbed her elbow with one hand, his grip steely and cruel. "Nice and slow. Straight ahead."

That voice, she thought, shuddering involuntarily as images of slime went through her mind. And that cologne—that horrible musky pine-scented cologne. Marianne struggled to remain calm. It wasn't easy.

There was a roaring in her ears. Her throat and mouth were so dry they ached. "Mr. Merchant, I presume?" she rasped, her heart pounding. *Killer and victim,* she thought. *This is how it felt, how Stan must have felt. Oh, god, I have to get out of here, have to....*

But until she could formulate a plan the only thing she could do was buy time. With questions, conversations, anything to slow him and the inevitable down.

"Very good," he said softly, his laughter low and grating and heinous against her ear. "I commend you on your power of observation."

Icy shudders racked her frame. "Where are we going?" Marianne managed unsteadily, swallowing around the knot of utter terror in her throat. *Keep him talking,* she thought. *Distracted. Learn as much as you can, while you can.*

"Back to the office. We'll do our business there."

His voice sounded so cold, merciless; she knew then he was going to kill her and that he'd have little if any regret. They passed a deserted ballroom, decorated eighteenth-century style, then a long corridor with many doors and with hatchets hanging on the walls. When the ride started, Marianne knew those doors would open and close, seemingly under their own ghostly power, but for now they were shut and silent. Deathly silent.

"Where's the camera?" she asked.

He made a short rude sound. And then she realized what a tremendous fool she had been. Anxiety and desperation washed over her in numbing waves. Again, she'd caught on far too late.

"There never was any camera, was there?" she said resentfully in growing fury and horror, her fear drifting down on her like an awful smothering weight. *Fool,* she chided herself, *you stupid fool. You walked right into his trap.* "This was all a setup." She stumbled and almost lost her footing completely. He grabbed her and yanked her upright, then pushed her on so roughly it was all she could do not to stumble again.

He wasn't answering her question. Suddenly, she could feel his fear, like a palpable force floating out around him, and for a moment hope leaped like a flame.

He cleared his throat and tried to reassert his authority. "Yeah, it was a way to meet you," he affirmed. "To find out what you knew and keep tabs on what was going on."

Marianne whirled to face him, feeling both furious and on the edge of hysteria, because it seemed to her the deeper they went in to the building, the closer she was to her grave. She had to clear her mind, to fight for time, for a plan. She wanted answers, too. "That night in my office," she reminded him roughly, remembering the lost child, the diversion. Tom had been there and then he'd left. He looked so disinterested now, as if on some level he'd already written her off. She fought to keep her voice steady. "Someone broke in." She remembered the bogus cleaning person she'd suspected of searching through her things. Had what he'd been after already been taken?

"I had a look around," Tom Merchant said flatly, from behind his beard.

She had nothing to lose. She might as well rattle him, too, Marianne thought. "Well, we're even then," she couldn't resist saying, a triumphant grin on her face. "Because I looked through your things, too."

Tom Merchant stopped walking and, grabbing the front of her blouse, knocked her up against the closest wall and slapped her face. Her ears rang with the impact and she moaned. He rammed the gun against her throat. "You what?" he asked through clenched teeth.

Her lip bleeding, she stared at him in growing fury and horror. She was desperate. She was scared. But she was looking for revenge. He might kill her, she thought, calming slightly, but he couldn't make her die a coward. He couldn't negate what she already knew, even if the best she could do was make him afraid for his life, too. After all, she'd already sensed his fear once. Who said she couldn't make him run? "I know the beard is fake," she said softly, emphatically, doing her best to disturb him into acting without thought, into running for his life, too. "I know about the cologne, about the credit card charged to the hilt . . ."

His skin took on a red, mottled look. He slapped her again, his triumphant smile fading to an ugly sneer. "What else do you know?" he asked, a murderous look in his eyes.

Marianne lifted her chin, tears of pain and indignation streaming down her face. *Bastard,* she thought. *I'll get the best of you yet.* "That you're connected with the KGB," she said with icy fury. "That what you're doing will put you in jail for a very long time. I know that you're framing an innocent man—Joe Maitland—and his family, trying to make them all look like spies. And that you or your friends killed Stan Howell—"

Merchant's face changed. He became uneasy, tense. "I had nothing to do with that."

Marianne let her tone turn vicious. "Well, your friends surely did."

"They're not my friends," he muttered resentfully.

"Then why are you helping them frame all these innocent people, myself included?" He didn't answer. "Admit it. You broke into my apartment and Doug's room. You planted that money in my closet and the tiny camera with the microfilm under his bed.''

His eyes glinted cruelly, but he didn't deny it. ''I wouldn't have had to do that if you'd minded your own business,'' he said furiously.

''And what was I supposed to do with all this violence happening here in my domain?''

''Let her go!''

The cold voice cut through their dialogue. Marianne turned to see Bryant Rockwell framed in the doorway, a revolver in his hand. He was alone, but he wasn't afraid. His expression was grim and commanding; indeed, he acted as if he were the only one with a gun, despite the fact Tom Merchant still held one at her throat.

Reacting on impulse, she tried to push free of Merchant. He kept the gun at her neck and grabbed a handful of hair, pulling on it viciously to hold her still. ''You're not going anywhere, honey,'' he drawled, yanking her back against his side.

''There's no reason to hurt her,'' Bryant dissented calmly, coldly.

''There's every reason!'' Merchant replied, never taking his eyes from the FBI man. He turned to Marianne momentarily. ''I ain't going to jail because of you, honey.''

''Look, all you have to do is tie her up. Leave the country. You've already framed her and the Maitlands. There's no reason to add murder to this.''

How much had Bryant heard? Marianne wondered, with a dizzying sense of relief. Or had he figured it out for himself? ·

Tom Merchant continued to stare at Bryant consideringly. The gun was pressing painfully into her throat.

"I can't let her go," he drawled finally, his voice dropping to a hoarse whisper. "She knows too much."

Marianne's arms and legs were shaking like leaves in the wind, but she was coherent enough to pick up on Merchant's sudden thick southern accent—an accent that had been successfully hidden up to that point. Looking into his face, she knew now why he looked so pale. And what the rice powder had probably been for. He'd wanted to hide the natural darkness of his skin, the golden brown hue that resulted from summers spent in the sun.

Who was this man, anyway? she wondered desperately, a sick acid taste welling up in her dry mouth. And where was he really from?

Bryant held his ground, the gun still pointed at his assailant. "You don't want to kill her," he repeated calmly. "Believe me, there is no need. So cut your losses now and hand her over to me."

Smiling at her fear, liking his power, Merchant moved the gun along the line of her collarbone. She knew then he wasn't going to do what Bryant said. She felt dizzy and sick with the depth of her fear—and deeply ashamed, for being fool enough to play right into his hands, right into her death. Suddenly, she had to know who he was and where he was from, if it was the last thing she ever did, and despite the gun at her throat, she reached up, grabbed the end of the beard and gave a hard yank.

Just as the beard pulled free, Bryant jumped into action and leaped forward, yelling, "Holden! Watch out!"

Too late, Marianne thought with satisfaction, tossing the ugly mat of dark blond hair to the floor. The beard was off.

Then Bryant's words sank in. He had called him Holden. Who the hell was Holden? She searched her brain frantically. And why had the words been voiced so affectionately and protectively when the two men were enemies? And then, looking up into the bare, startled face of Tom Merchant alias Holden, Marianne saw the resemblance between the two men. The familial resemblance. And then she knew—they were brothers.

"You're the one who owns the nightclubs in Atlanta," she murmured, looking up into Holden's murderous rage.

She glanced at Bryant. "And you—you're in on this, too!"

Bryant swore, quickly crossing to Marianne's side. "You stupid bitch."

"You just sealed your fate," Holden muttered, tightening his grasp on her hair, and giving it a brutally hard jerk. Her brain told her to run, but even as she thought about trying it she looked down into the barrel of the gun, the two-against-one odds, and knew she'd never make it three feet. He wouldn't hesitate to shoot. In fact, she realized with horrifying clarity, he'd probably take great delight in it.

"Start walking," Bryant said, flanking her on one side. Holden was on the other. They started up the staircase. Marianne thought she knew where they were going—to the security office and control room on the third floor. The guard was there, and probably whoever else they'd managed to apprehend.

"Why, Bryant? Why are you doing this?" He didn't respond and she finished deprecatingly, amazed again at how wrong she had been about him. "I never thought you were a crook."

"I'm not. I'm an opportunist."

"There's a difference?"

His eyes were dull, expressionless. He looked very tired suddenly, almost beaten. "Yeah, I think so." He shrugged, and continued, suddenly wanting her to understand. "The Russians have been stealing our technology for years. It's a well-known fact they'll buy anything they can get their hands on." Half his mouth lifted in a knowing grin. "So I decided to sell them secrets, too."

Her pulse was racing again. As long as Bryant was there, she had a chance to come out of this alive. A slim one, maybe, but a chance nonetheless. "FBI secrets?"

She saw the confidence grow in him and his grin broadened speculatively. "Darling, I said I wanted to make money, not get thrown in jail for treason."

She puzzled over what he meant, and decided finally that stealing from the FBI must have violated his very strange and individual code of ethics. "So you stole from others," she guessed slowly, aware the flaccid feeling had returned in her knees. "The Navy?"

"No. I enlisted the help of others with security clearances. I told them the FBI and the CIA were setting up traps to catch spies. And they needed authentic-looking but ultimately worthless documents to sell to the spies. The FBI, or I, would pay them handsomely for their work, but it had to be top secret."

"You recruited Pam and Seth." Marianne took the steps as slowly as possible, but they were already on the third flight.

"Right."

"As well as me," Holden said grimly.

"Hey, I needed someone to make the deals," Bryant defended himself. "Someone subject to that kind of temptation. And with your nightclubs in trouble, you about to bail out anyway—''

Holden made no comment. Marianne could tell he'd once considered the idea a stroke of genius; now, though, he was having his doubts.

"You went to Europe to make the deals," Marianne guessed.

Holden looked at Bryant, his eyes grim and compelling. "I told you she knew too much."

"Only something went wrong," Marianne theorized slowly. "And the spies realized they'd been duped. So they came looking for you." She turned to Holden, realizing from the anger on his face it was true. She thought about Pam getting sick in the Mexican restaurant the moment the spies had walked in the door. "And Seth and Pam."

Bryant looked at his brother. "I thought the new identity I set up for you was iron-clad, mistake-proof."

"Only it wasn't," Marianne said. "And they demanded the real stuff. Did they do the same to Pam and Seth, too?"

Bryant nodded slowly, reluctantly.

"Then his hand in the car door—''

"Was done by the KGB. Deliberately. Pam watched. They told her to consider it a warning."

"And she came down here to deal again. Only by then her dad was on to it."

"Right. He and Stan intercepted the drop last Sunday in the International Bazaar."

"What happened to the stolen technology?"

"It hasn't been seen since," Holden said grimly. His eyes looked murderous again.

Marianne thought of Pam and Seth locked in their hotel room, forced to work with the spies. "So Seth and

Pam made up a third batch of documents? To be delivered—''

''Marianne? Where are you?'' Suddenly Doug's voice echoed through the empty building, cutting off her question.

Marianne froze, feeling a renewed sense of desperation and protectiveness. She loved Doug and didn't want to see him hurt. It was enough she was involved in this. ''Let him go.'' She grabbed Bryant's arm.

''We can't.''

Holden jabbed the gun into Marianne's ribs, and his fingers dug painfully into her arm. ''Call him,'' he ordered roughly. ''And tell him to come up here. Do it now!''

Knowing she had no choice, Marianne complied reluctantly. ''Doug!'' she yelled, her voice cracking weakly. ''Third floor!''

Seconds later, Doug was running lightly up the steps. Marianne saw him for the first time as he rounded the landing and tried to call out a warning but it was too late.

''Welcome,'' Holden said.

Doug saw Marianne with the gun to her throat. He turned white, then red, and every muscle in his body tensed.

''That's it,'' Bryant continued, picking up where his brother left off. ''Nice and easy. Come on up and join us and no funny stuff now or you're both going to end up dead.'' Marianne held on to the hope that Bryant's sensible streak would prevail.

Doug complied. As he neared her his eyes met Marianne's. He seemed to need reassurance she was all right. She let him know with a small nod that she was, even if she was scared out of her skin.

"Hurt her," Doug muttered to Bryant and Holden under his breath, "and I'll personally kill you both."

Holden was the first to laugh. "That'll be the day. No, if anyone dies here, buddy, you will."

"Wrong again, comrades," said yet another voice from the shadows, this one from behind them. They turned in unison, to see a swarthy man with a compact machine gun walking toward them. "Because now you are all dead."

A second man, blond and slim, also came up from the rear, and just that easily, the four of them were surrounded. As Marianne watched in horror, the two KGB men closed in.

## Chapter Sixteen

The two Russians were both wearing suits, clearly getting ready to make their final getaway. But first they would have to tie up all the loose ends, get rid of the witnesses, and that meant murder.

Marianne felt sick. Sick and weak. Doug reached over and grabbed her hand, telling her with his touch that it was going to be all right. She only wished she could be sure it would work out the way he intended.

"Put down your weapons," the swarthy one ordered.

Knowing when he was outmatched, Bryant did as ordered. Not Holden. Fool that he was, he ducked behind Marianne and tried to outshoot them. Doug shouted and hit the floor, pulling Marianne underneath him. The blasts made muffled pinging sounds as the bullets whizzed by, and then Holden was down, too, blood oozing from a wound in his shoulder, another in the back of his thigh.

The swarthy Russian stood stock-still, a murderous look on his face. He was all too ready to use the gun again. Suddenly everything fell into place for Marianne. "You killed Stan, didn't you?" she accused.

The thin one confirmed it. "Just as we will kill you. Now get up."

Weakly, they complied, with Doug holding her hand once again.

The gesture wasn't lost on the swarthy man, who sneered contemptuously at the hopeless chivalry and romanticism.

"In there," the thin blond agent ordered, using the tip of the machine gun to point to the office door.

A lump of terror in her throat, Marianne went first, followed by Doug and Bryant. Holden was hauled in after them, and flung facedown in a corner. He groaned at the impact, then lapsed mercifully into oblivion, as Bryant bent over him, trying to stop the bleeding. In the office were the guard who had called Marianne, Pam and Seth. They were tied up, blindfolded and gagged.

The swarthy agent handed his gun to the blond man. From the inside of his suit he pulled a small, slim case filled with syringes. Doug was directed to stand against the far wall, next to Pam and Seth, and away from Marianne. He went reluctantly, his eyes on her face. Despite everything, she knew he was telling her he loved her and that he would do his best to get them out of this, as would she.

"Truth serum?" Bryant said grimly, standing.

"We want to know everything before we go," the thin man said.

Marianne looked around. The door to the adjacent storeroom was open and her eyes fell on the cleaning cart just inside. She could see several gallon cans of wax on the bottom rack.

Catching her looking that way, the thin man closed the door. Marianne tried not to show her disappointment: the cans of cleaner might have proved valuable weapons.

"So you can clear up more loose ends?" Bryant scoffed.

"Must be the same stuff they gave Stan," Doug added. "Only none of us is going to take a swim afterward."

"You only wish," said the blond man mysteriously, malice in his eyes.

A shudder went down Marianne's spine at the implication. She wanted to run, but her feet felt cemented to the floor.

Without warning, the thin KGB agent raised the butt end of his rifle and smacked it into Doug's jaw. The impact sent Doug reeling, but he didn't make a sound. "We will tell you when to talk," the swarthy man advised irritably, advancing on Bryant, the needle primed.

Trying to move as unobtrusively as possible, Marianne edged back toward the door. To the side of the light switch was a small panel that contained the level to activate the haunted house. "Hurry up," the swarthy man commanded, as Bryant fiddled with his sleeve.

"I'm hurrying," Bryant said, and then sarcastically, still stalling for time, he asked, "any of this bring back pleasant memories, Marianne?"

"So you're the ones who nabbed her off the Space City ride," Doug murmured.

"With Tom Merchant's help," the swarthy man admitted calmly.

The time it took to utter that sentence was all the leeway Marianne needed to throw the light switch and send the third floor into total blackness. As she moved Doug kicked the gun out of the thin man's hand. It fell and skidded across the floor. Her heart slamming against her ribs, Marianne yanked open the box and pulled as hard as she could on the lever.

There was nothing, just total blackness.

She pulled again and ran. She knew their best chance was to get help.

Her heart pumping frantically in her chest, she raced down the long hallway and leaped down the steps. Gasping, she rounded the corner. She slid into the second room on the left and felt for a metal box. It swung open and she pulled on the lever. The house exploded with a cacophony of eerie music, howls and screams, the sounds of doors opening and shutting automatically, the slicing sound of a guillotine coming down, the motorized sounds of the ride.

The sound of a witch cackling evilly made the hair on her arms stand on end. In an effort to get away from the disturbing sound, she raced silently down the corridor, and then walked right into a thick, silky web. She almost screamed as the lifelike rubber tarantula moved against her cheek.

She got down on all fours and crawled beneath the silky web, which extended the full width of the hall. Ignoring the distant sounds of howling coyotes and bloodcurdling screams, she went as far as she was able through the connecting rooms, then decided she had to go out via the main route. She knew from the way the house was set up electrically that the men wouldn't be able to activate the inner lights unless they first turned off the ride. As long as the ride was going, she had the cover of darkness.

Easing the door open, she glanced in the hall, saw a hatchet moving up and down, a witch flying in and out, appearing to dance with ghostly vision in midair, and a spreading stain that looked like blood appearing and disappearing on the opposite wall.

That was it, Marianne thought. She needed a weapon and a costume—something to defend herself with and something to help her blend in with the scenery.

Grabbing a hooded black cape from a dummy sitting next to a bed, she pulled the camouflaging cloth around her and tucked her red hair beneath the hood. She wrested a fake ax from the wall and eased into the hallway again. She heard the sound of a scuffle several rooms away, and then a man's cry of pain. It sounded like Bryant. Had he been killed?

Oh, God, where were they? Would she ever get out of here alive?

Knowing time was of the essence, she forced herself to proceed, moving farther down the hall, not toward the exit, as they would expect, but back, in the direction they had all come.

She approached another juncture of the hall, where the ride came up. She paused, breathing slowly and cautiously, remembering what she knew about the route. Visitors were pulled through the building on a slow-moving train of black spider-shaped cars. Getting into one of the cars would be the fastest way down, and the most obvious.

She tiptoed closer, her heart pounding, to see what she could of the floor beneath. On the first floor was the ballroom, where a piano was playing by itself. Ghosts dressed in eighteenth-century garb were dancing the waltz, going around and around. Only something was wrong. In the middle of the room covered with centuries of dust, a man was moving slowly and Bryant was down on the floor, clutching his middle.

Where was Doug? Where was the tall, thin man?

She wavered on the edge of fear, unable to decide what to do.

Marianne saw the thin man coming up in a car, some eight feet to her left. She ducked back against the wall, turning sideways, and raised the ax. Behaving as if she were a mechanical ghost, she lowered the ax once and then again, her manner very precise. He looked past her, failing to realize she was real and not just one of the ghostly mannequins in the house.

As soon as she was sure the thin man was gone, Marianne tiptoed to the edge again and peered over the passing cars to the juncture of floors beneath. She swore inwardly. The swarthy man was gone.

Marianne hopped onto the ride and huddled down on the floor. She remained there until the ride hit the first floor and leveled off, preparing to go through the first-floor exhibits, before heading to the exit.

*Almost there,* she thought. *Almost.*

She felt him first, moving behind her. Whirling, she faced the swarthy man with the gun. Acting purely on instinct she rushed at him, tackling him around the knees.

The move surprised him and he fell backward, striking his head on the metal train track. The next car bumped into him, stopping automatically as it encountered the resistance of his skull. He was unconscious, his head partially caught under the wheel. One down, one to go, Marianne thought victoriously, adrenaline pumping in her veins.

Knowing she had no time to spare, Marianne raced off, heading for the dark, narrow hallway where a skeleton in top hat and tails sat playing a haunting rendition of "The Wedding March." The bride was almost breathtakingly beautiful, but the groom had no face.

When they turned every few seconds to kiss, Marianne shuddered and could barely contain the shiver that slid down her spine.

Checking to the right and left, she edged toward the door. The ride had started to move again—which meant the swarthy man had recovered, or his body had been moved.

Either possibility was deadly. Not breaking stride, Marianne kept going. The next room was what had once been a vast dining hall. Specters floated above her, laughing maniacally, while mechanical snakes slithered across the floor. Marianne barely avoided stepping on one of them and again she had to resist the impulse to scream.

Marianne hurried her steps, breaking in to a dead run. Then suddenly the tall thin man appeared in front of her, blood running down his jaw. He'd lost his gun; instead, he carried a syringe. Marianne slid to a halt, then began involuntarily backing away. "No," she whispered defiantly, raising her rubber hatchet. She was damned if she'd let him do this to her again.

He smiled and gave chase. Marianne darted past him and retaliated with a blood-curdling scream. Anything to bring help. She'd almost made it to the exit before he grabbed her and, hooking an ankle beneath her feet, knocked her off balance and wrestled her to the floor.

The parquet was layered with a thick gray powder made to resemble centuries of dust. As they rolled, both grappling for the needle, the dust got in their eyes, burning terribly, temporarily blinding them both. Marianne shoved the palm of her hand beneath his nose and rammed her fingers into his eyes. He screamed with pain and blindly stabbed the needle. It caught on the fabric of her sleeve, went through her blouse to her skin.

Before Marianne could even react, Doug was there, pulling the man up by the lapels and throwing him back down on the floor, ramming his head against the thick wooden planks.

"Are you all right?" Doug asked, helping her to her feet. Blood spilled from his nose and a cut beneath his eye.

But he was in one piece. They were alive.

Marianne nodded, threw her arms around his neck and hugged him tight. "Where's Bryant?"

"Still unconscious. In the ballroom. With the looks of the bump on his head he'll be out for some time."

She drew back urgently. "We've got to get help. The others—"

"The Russian is tied up, too. I found him and used his belt and tie."

Marianne sagged against him, her relief profound. They really *were* going to be okay. It seemed unbelievable. And then he was holding her so tightly she could barely breathe. She'd never felt anything more wonderful in her life.

DOUG AND MARIANNE were both there when Joe was released from the Cypress City jail early Thursday morning. It had been a long night for them. But with the new day came the end of the chaos and the happy resolution the Maitland family had been hoping for.

"Son," Joe said, taking Doug into his arms for a hard embrace. "Thank God you're all right." He hugged him tighter, for a moment unwilling or unable to let go. "I heard what happened." He released his son slowly, tears of pride and gratitude in his eyes. And Marianne knew, if there had ever been any doubt, that

Joe Maitland loved and respected his son tremendously.

"I'm proud of you, son." He turned to Marianne and hugged her, too. "And you, too, young woman. I hear you've been quite a help to my son. Hell, my entire family."

"I tried." Marianne smiled.

Pam and Seth walked forward to embrace Joe, too. Both had been shaken up, but unharmed by the ordeal. Their baby was doing fine, too. Billy was last to greet his father. Then arm in arm, the family walked out of the small police station and into the morning sunlight.

"Keel says you're going to get an award," Doug said to his dad.

"Yeah. For helping the FBI get enough to convict the two KGB men you apprehended."

"They're going to honor Stan, too."

"He's getting the Navy Cross for extraordinary heroism in action against an armed enemy."

"I'm proud of you, Dad. What you did took real guts."

"Even though you didn't follow written procedure and check in with your commanding officer first," Commander Keel added, coming up to join the group. "Congratulations, Joe," he said, holding out his hand. "You're a real hero."

The two men paused to size up each other. Doug could see a truce in the works there, too. Whatever differences Keel and his father had had seemed to have passed. "On the job as well as off?" Joe asked.

Keel nodded slowly. "I can't say I wish you hadn't gone about this more circumspectly. But what the hell, you got the job done."

"And that's all that counts," Billy said.

"Maybe," Keel allowed. "At any rate, you're one lucky man, Joe, to have a family who cares about you so much."

"I am lucky," Joe admitted. "Very lucky." He looked around at the group and then turned back to Doug. For the first time, Doug saw the true respect in his father's eyes he'd always hungered for. And he knew this once he hadn't let Joe down.

For the first time in years, Doug felt completely at peace with himself and his father. Maybe it was true what they said. Something good did come out of everything.

Pam was relieved to know both of the Russians were in a military jail, under heavy guard, awaiting trial. "We never meant to do anything remotely treasonous," she explained to the group in general, recounting what they'd already told to the authorities. "The way Bryant explained it to us, we were going to be helping him trap spies. Not aiding and abetting them."

Seth sighed. "Yeah. Strange as it sounds, I think this was all Bryant's idea of the perfect yuppie prank—the ultimate irony."

"I'll tell you one thing. Next time I won't be in such a rush to do my patriotic duty in an unofficial manner," Pam said. "We never thought it would lead to such chaos. We only wanted to earn some extra money, so we could pay off our debts. But then Bryant double-crossed the Russians, and it all got out of hand. We were scared for our lives."

"We had no choice but to cooperate, but even then we didn't betray our country," Seth added.

"They know you didn't give away any real confidential information," Commander Keel reassured them, "even the last time."

Billy nodded. "I picked up the Misty Mouse doll. The authorities have that. And they expect to eventually get full confessions from Bryant and Holden Rockwell. Evidently, they're trying to cut some sort of a deal with the prosecutors as we speak."

"They're going to go free?" Joe seemed to disapprove.

Keel shrugged. "Probably not, Joe, though that's up to the justice department. But I imagine they will be given some leniency because of their cooperation. It's pretty clear just from what I heard of the interrogation last night that Bryant never meant to actually betray his country. He was just trying to earn some easy money to help his brother out and at the same time put something over on some of the spies who'd infiltrated this country, maybe teach them a lesson or maybe prevent them from doing this again. But then it all got way out of hand."

Marianne added, "I think Holden would've killed me if Bryant hadn't been there to stop him."

There was a silence. Nina, who'd tagged along with Craig Keel, said, "I know what it is to be afraid. To be caught up in something that just gets out of hand."

Marianne looked at her boss. "I never did thank you for sending in the troops last night." Nina had found out where Marianne had gone and sent the CWR security force over to the Haunted House. They'd arrived just as she and Doug had started to call the Cypress City police.

Nina had also had a long talk with Marianne at the police station, explaining how she had been living under a new identity since coming to work at Children's World, and how afraid she had been of being exposed.

Marianne had finally understood her boss's standoff-ishness, and she had vowed to keep Nina's secret.

Nina smiled. "I admit I was reluctant to get involved, even peripherally, with anything criminal. I was afraid I would be drawn into it and be in danger. So I let Marianne take the heat. But when I saw she was in danger, too, I couldn't stand by."

"I heard you were down here pretty fast," Joe said to Commander Keel.

Keel smiled and sent Doug an approving glance. "You can thank your son for that, Joe. He was the one who alerted me that something was up. You weren't underground twenty-four hours before he was calling the NIS headquarters, fishing around for information about you and Stan. You two hadn't been very productive lately with your assigned work. That, coupled with the fact the two of you were always busy and preoccupied night and day—and often unreachable to boot—told me something was up. So I decided to see what I could do."

"One thing is bothering me," Marianne said, "if they went to such great lengths to frame the entire family, why didn't they ever call it in?"

"I think they were going to," Commander Keel said, "but not until after they'd left the country. They didn't want the press latching on to that until they were safely out of reach. I've got to admit it was a good ruse. Bryant had been dropping some hints to me—very subtly, and almost accidentally the past week—hoping, I think, to lead me in that direction. I admit I wondered about it, especially with all the leaks in Navy security of recent weeks. But the CIA tells me they've traced that back to another source now, one greatly removed from the Maitlands."

"So, you thought I might be a spy?" Joe said, giving his superior a skeptical, testing look.

"I've never pretended to understand you, Joe," Craig said, extending his hand. "Until now."

Joe shook Keel's hand. "I think it's time we started working together."

"Well, I'm just glad it's all over." Pam sighed.

"Right," Marianne said brightly. "All you have to do now is finish out the rest of your vacation."

Her comment was rewarded with a chorus of groans.

"Afraid not," Billy said, straightening his hat. "I'm due back on my ship tomorrow night. I've got the first plane out this afternoon."

"And we've got some explaining to do to our employers," Pam said, glancing at Seth.

Joe was equally apologetic. "Much as I'd like to stay on in Florida and have the vacation I missed, I've got a lot to do in Washington."

Keel nodded. "Maybe we can fly back together, Joe."

"I'd like that, sir."

Marianne turned to Doug. "I've got a flight out later tonight, too," he said softly. "I've got a recording session early tomorrow. It's not something I can reschedule."

Disappointment wafted through her in waves. "I understand." With effort, she kept her voice cheerful and civil as she looked at Doug. It seemed impossible they might be saying goodbye. After all they'd been through...after all they'd come to mean to each other... Suddenly, she couldn't let him go, not without a chance to say a more personal farewell.

"Got time for one last tour of the park?" she asked lightly. "I know you didn't get to see much of it while you were here."

He didn't hesitate to accept her offer. "I'd like that very much."

"THE SPACE CITY RIDE wasn't the same the second time around," Doug said, looping his arm casually around Marianne's shoulders.

"Not as much excitement."

"Oh, I don't know about that," he said, tightening his grip on her possessively and slanting her a roguish grin. "But it was certainly much safer."

They looked over the sides of the ski lift they were riding in. He seemed to be searching for something to say. "The park is big, isn't it?"

Marianne nodded. She knew how he felt. She felt miserable inside, too, but she was trying her best to make these last few hours together happy ones.

He knitted his brows together thoughtfully. "I could probably come back here two—three times a year, and still not use it all."

"Probably." She focused on his face, committing everything about him to memory. She would miss looking into those kind silver eyes and looking at that untamed thatch of wheat blond hair. She would miss sleeping with him, making love with him, waking to find his arms wrapped securely around her, even talking to him on the phone whenever the urge struck.

With a sigh, she realized she'd been right to think her life would never be the same after Doug. It wouldn't be.

"How would you feel about me coming back?" he asked slowly.

"I'd like that very much." But Marianne wanted more, too.

"You like your job here, don't you?"

"Yeah, I do."

"It took you a long time to work your way up to senior manager?"

"Years."

He nodded.

"Not much session work in Florida, is there?" she asked.

"No. Next to none, actually."

"Playing in concert year round here—"

"Would get boring for the guests as well as the musicians. No, that wouldn't work."

He looked at her seriously, all the love he felt for her reflected in his eyes. "How much time off do you get a year?"

She knew how he felt; she was beginning to feel desperate to somehow find a way to make this work, no matter what the sacrifices. It was encouraging to realize he felt the same. "Three weeks."

"Think you might make it out to L.A.?"

"Yes," she said softly, knowing she would find the time if it killed her.

"Good." He bent and kissed her, the caress long and slow and deep. It ended only when the ride ended. Tourists chuckled around them, and then someone snickered, "That's newlyweds for you." Marianne only wished.

"Well, I'm going to have to get going if I want to make my plane." Doug took her hand and began walking toward the monorail lines.

And then it hit her. Marianne realized finally this was it. It had been an incredible experience, spending the last ten days with Doug Maitland, unraveling the mystery of his father's disappearance, but now it was back to reality. And they were landing with a thud. They had separate lives, and like it or not, they had to get back to them.

Doug was quiet as they rode the monorail over to the hotel parking lot. Marianne had arranged for his luggage to be moved to his rental car in his absence. All that was left was the drive to the airport. She knew they were dragging out his goodbye but she didn't care.

"Mind if I kiss you one last time?" Doug asked unevenly.

She looked up at him, tears sparkling in her eyes. "I'd hate it if you didn't," she whispered softly.

His mouth met hers. The kiss wasn't passionate or sad. Instead it seemed to sum up everything he felt about her. She returned the emotion, letting him know how much she cared, how much she wanted, how much he had come to mean to her in so little time.

He released her slowly, all the love he felt for her on his face. Marianne knew it was now or never. She had to say goodbye or break down entirely and embarrass them both.

"Call me," she said, using every bit of willpower she had to keep her voice calm.

He nodded, his eyes holding hers. "And you do the same."

"I will." Her throat aching, Marianne started to walk away. She'd gone maybe two steps when the tears she'd been holding back welled up in her eyes and spilled over her lashes, coursing like a stream down her face. She'd always hated goodbyes, but this was the worst parting she'd ever had to endure.

And why? Because suddenly their plans to see each other all sounded so lame. This wasn't at all what either of them wanted. And they both knew it.

Yes, here in Florida, she had her job. But a job didn't love her back. A job didn't keep her warm at night, or laugh with her, or help her through the troubled times. Her job didn't listen to her pour out her innermost feelings. Only Doug could do those things for her.

She turned back.

He was already walking toward her, a lopsided grin on his face. "I don't want to go, either," he said hoarsely.

And she knew then that if they wanted it badly enough, they could find a way to make this love of theirs work.

"I could get a job in California. Maybe it wouldn't be what I'm doing now, but maybe it's time I had a change."

"No. You've got an important job here. If anyone's going to move, it'll be me."

"But your session work—"

"I'll fly back and forth. Believe me, Marianne, we can get this worked out. Hell, who knows, maybe I'll even be able to find people interested in recording down here."

"You really mean it, don't you?" Tears of happiness glistened in her eyes.

"Do I look like the kind of guy who'd walk away from the best thing that ever happened to him?" He hugged her close and rambled on about concessions they both could make.

She knew then that it would work. "I love you," she said, standing on tiptoe and lacing her arms around his neck.

"And I love you."

Marianne smiled. "Then it's settled. We'll have a future together," she said softly. Finally, she had it all, they both did. There'd be no more living out of a suitcase for him, no more lonely nights for her. Only unity, a sense of family, a closeness no physical separation could ever touch.

Doug smiled, and held her closer still. "One for all and all for one," he murmured tenderly, kissing her again.

Marianne met his gaze seriously. "And the best is yet to come," she agreed softly, thinking they were very, very lucky indeed.

# Temptation™

## TEMPTATION WILL BE EVEN HARDER TO RESIST...

In September, Temptation is presenting a sophisticated new face to the world. A fresh look that truly brings Harlequin's most intimate romances into focus.

What's more, all-time favorite authors Barbara Delinsky, Rita Clay Estrada, Jayne Ann Krentz and Vicki Lewis Thompson will join forces to help us celebrate. The result? A very special quartet of Temptations...

- **Four striking covers**
- **Four stellar authors**
- **Four sensual love stories**
- **Four variations on one spellbinding theme**

All in one great month! Give in to Temptation in September.

TDESIGN-1

**Lynda Ward's**

# LEAP THE MOON

... the continuing saga of *The Welles Family*

You've already met Elaine Welles, the oldest daughter of powerful tycoon Burton Welles, in Superromance #317, *Race the Sun*. You cheered her on as she threw off the shackles of her heritage and won the love of her life, Ruy de Areias.

Now it's her sister's turn. Jennie Welles is the drop-dead-gorgeous, most rebellious Welles sister, and she's determined to live life her way—and flaunt it in her father's face.

When she meets Griffin Stark, however, she learns there's more to life than glamour and independence. She learns about kindness, compassion and sharing. One nagging question remains: is she good enough for a man like Griffin? Her father certainly doesn't think so....

*Leap the Moon* . . . a Harlequin Superromance coming to you in August. Don't miss it!

## *Harlequin American Romance*®

# JOIN THE CELEBRATION!
# THE FIFTH ANNIVERSARY
# OF HARLEQUIN
# AMERICAN ROMANCE

1988 is a banner year for Harlequin American
Romance—it marks our fifth anniversary.

For five successful years we've been bringing you
heartwarming, exciting romances, but we're not
stopping there. In August, 1988, we've got an
extraspecial treat for you. Join us next month when we
feature four of American Romance's best—and four
favorite—authors.

Judith Arnold, Rebecca Flanders, Beverly Sommers
and Anne Stuart will enchant you with the stories of
four women friends who lived in the same New York
apartment building and whose lives, one by one, take an
unexpected turn. Meet Abbie, Jaime, Suzanne and
Marielle—the women of YORKTOWN TOWERS.

Four believable American Romance heroines...four
contemporary American women just like you...by four
of your favorite American Romance authors.

Don't miss these special stories.
Enjoy the fifth-anniversary
celebration of Harlequin
American Romance!

HAR5-1